Old Roads, New Roads

Ruskin Bond is known for his signature simplistic and witty writing style. He is the author of several bestselling short stories, novellas, collections, essays and children's books and has contributed a number of poems and articles to various magazines and anthologies. At the age of twenty-three, he won the prestigious John Llewellyn Rhys Prize for his first novel, *The Room on the Roof*. He was also the recipient of the Padma Shri in 1999, Lifetime Achievement Award by the Delhi Government in 2012 and the Padma Bhushan in 2014.

Born in 1934, Ruskin Bond grew up in Jamnagar, Shimla, New Delhi and Dehradun. Apart from three years in the UK, he has spent all his life in India, and now lives in Landour, Mussoorie, with his adopted family.

RUSKIN BOND
Old Roads, New Roads

Published by
Rupa Publications India Pvt. Ltd 2023
161-B/4, Gulmohar House,
Yusuf Sarai Community Centre,
New Delhi 110049

Sales centres:
Bengaluru Chennai
Hyderabad Kolkata Mumbai

Copyright © Ruskin Bond 2023

This is a work of fiction. Names, characters, places and incidents are either the product of the author's imagination or are used fictitiously and any resemblance to any actual person, living or dead, events or locales is entirely coincidental.

All rights reserved.
No part of this publication may be reproduced, transmitted, or stored in a retrieval system, in any form or by any means, electronic, mechanical, photocopying, recording or otherwise, without the prior permission of the publisher.

P-ISBN: 978-93-5702-211-8
E-ISBN: 978-93-5702-213-2

Fourth impression 2025

10 9 8 7 6 5 4

The moral right of the author has been asserted.

Printed in India

This book is sold subject to the condition that it shall not, by way of trade or otherwise, be lent, resold, hired out, or otherwise circulated, without the publisher's prior consent, in any form of binding or cover other than that in which it is published.

CONTENTS

Introduction vii

1. Cold Beer at Chutmalpur 1
2. The Break of Monsoon in Meerut 7
3. Footloose in Agra 11
4. On The Delhi Road 20
5. Sacred Shrines Along the Way 27
6. Breakfast Time 38
7. The Open Road 42
8. All About My Walkabouts 45
9. Picnic at Fox Burn 49
10. The Road to Anjani Sain 54
11. The Grand Trunk Road 58
12. Running Away 64
13. Walking the Streets of Delhi 82
14. Street of The Red Well 91
15. The Road to Badrinath 95
16. A Night Walk Home 103
17. The Walkers' Club 107

INTRODUCTION

One often hears of the journey and the destination being at odds with each other—one can either enjoy the journey or be excited about reaching the destination. For a long time, I used to believe that the journey is more important than the destination, but, looking back, I realize that I have enjoyed both just as much. There are few feelings in the world better than staring out the window while travelling down a winding mountain road, basking in the warm glow of the early morning sun as the crisp, cool air smelling of evergreen forests whips through your hair. At the same time, there is a unique joy and excitement to exploring a new destination—meeting interesting people, eating delicious food and wandering around unexplored mohallas of quaint old towns.

In *Old Roads, New Roads*, I have put together stories, like 'On the Delhi Road' and 'The Open Road', that make a case for enjoying the journey. At the same time, other stories, like 'Footloose in Agra' and 'The Break of Monsoon in Meerut', reveal the joys of exploring a destination, including chance encounters with all sorts of interesting people—from Hosain Ali of Agra whose stunning kites are said to have magical qualities to Mr P of Meerut who provided us much-needed shelter on a rainy day.

I hope this book of journeys to and from the hills, across

towns big and small, meeting wise and amusing people, inspires you to step out into the great outdoors and explore old roads and new ones for yourself!

Ruskin Bond

COLD BEER AT CHUTMALPUR

Just outside the small market town of Chutmalpur (on the way back from Delhi) one is greeted by a large signboard with just two words on it: Cold Beer. The signboard is almost as large as the shop from which the cold beer is dispensed; but after a gruelling five-hour drive from Delhi, in the heat and dust of May, a glass of chilled beer is welcome—except, of course, to teetotallers who will find other fizzy ways to satiate their thirst.

Chutmalpur is not the sort of place you'd choose to retire in. But it has its charms, not the least of which is its Sunday Market, when the varied produce of the rural interior finds its way on to the dusty pavements, and the air vibrates with noise, colour and odours. Carpets of red chillies, seasonal fruits, stacks of grain and vegetables, cheap toys for the children, bangles of lac, wooden artifacts, colourful underwear, sweets of every description, *churan* to go with them...

'*Lakar hajam, gather hajam!*' cries the churan-seller. Translated: digest wood, digest stones! That is, if you partake of this particular digestive pill which, when I tried it, appeared to be one part hing (asafoetida) and one part gunpowder. Things are seldom what they seem to be. Passing through the small town of Purkazi, I noticed a signboard which announced the availability of 'Books'—just that. Intrigued, I stopped to find out more about this bookshop in the wilderness. Perhaps I'd find a rare tome to add to my library. Peeping in, I discovered that the dark interior was stacked from floor to ceiling with exercise books! Apparently the shop owner was the supplier for the district.

Rare books can be seen in Roorkee, in the university's old library. Here, not many years ago, a First Folio Shakespeare turned up and was celebrated in the Indian press as a priceless discovery. Perhaps it's still there.

Also in the library is a bust of Sir Proby Cautley, who conceived and built the Ganga Canal, which starts at Haridwar and passes through Roorkee on its way across the Doab. Hardly anyone today has heard of Cautley, and yet surely his achievement outstrips that of many Englishmen in India—soldiers and statesmen who became famous for doing all the wrong things.

Cautley's Canal

Cautley came to India at the age of seventeen and joined the Bengal Artillery. In 1825, he assisted Captain Robert Smith, the engineer in charge of constructing the Eastern Yamuna Canal. By 1836 he was Superintendent-General of Canals. From the start, he worked towards his dream of building a Ganga Canal, and spent six months walking and riding through the jungles and countryside, taking each level and measurement himself, sitting up all night to transfer them to his maps. He was confident that a 500-kilometre canal was feasible. There were many objections and obstacles to his project, most of them financial, but Cautley persevered and eventually persuaded the East India Company to back him.

Digging for the canal began in 1839. Cautley had to make his own bricks—millions of them—his own brick kiln, and his own mortar. A hundred thousand tonnes of lime went into the mortar, the other main ingredient of which was *surkhi*, made by grinding over-burnt bricks to a powder. To reinforce the mortar, *ghur*, ground lentils and jute fibres were added to it.

Initially, opposition came from the priests in Haridwar, who felt that the waters of the holy Ganga would be imprisoned. Cautley pacified them by agreeing to leave a narrow gap in the dam through which the river water could flow unchecked. He won over the priests when he inaugurated his project with *aarti*, and the worship of Ganesh, the god of good beginnings. He also undertook the repair of the sacred bathing ghats along the river. The canal banks were also to have their own ghats with steps leading down to the water.

The headworks of the canal are at Haridwar, where the Ganga enters the plains after completing its majestic journey through the Himalayas. Below Haridwar, Cautley had to dig new courses for some of the mountain torrents that threatened the canal. He collected them into four steams and took them over the canal by means of four passages. Near Roorkee, the land fell away sharply and there Cautley had to build an aqueduct, a masonry bridge that carries the canal for half a kilometre across the Solani torrent—a unique engineering feat. At Roorkee, the canal is twenty-five metres higher than the parent river which flows almost parallel to it.

Most of the excavation work on the canal was done mainly by the Oads, a gypsy tribe who were professional diggers for most of northwest India. They took great pride in their work. Though extremely poor, Cautley found them a happy and carefree lot who worked in a very organized manner.

When the canal was formally opened on the 8 April 1854, its main channel was 348 miles long, its branches 306 and the distributaries over 3,000. Over 7,67,000 acres in 5,000 villages were irrigated. One of its main branches re-entered the Ganga at Kanpur; it also had branches to Fatehgarh, Bulandshahr and Aligarh.

Cautley's achievements did not end there. He was also actively involved in Dr Falconer's fossil expedition in the Siwaliks. He presented to the British Museum an extensive collection of fossil mammalia—including hippopotamus and crocodile fossils, evidence that the region was once swamp land or an inland sea. Other animal remains found there included the sabre-toothed tiger; Elephis ganesa, an elephant with a trunk ten-and-a-half feet long; a three-toed ancestor of the horse; the bones of a fossil ostrich; and the remains of giant cranes and tortoises. Exciting times, exciting finds.

Nor did Cautley's interests and activities end in fossil excavation. My copy of Surgeon General Balfour's *Cyclopaedia of India* (1873) lists a number of fascinating reports and papers by Cautley. He wrote on a submerged city, twenty feet underground, near Behut in the Doab; on the coal and lignite in the Himalayas; on gold washings in the Siwalik Hills, between the Yamuna and Sutlej rivers; on a new species of snake; on the mastodons of the Siwaliks; on the manufacture of tar; and on *Panchukkis* or corn mills.

How did he find time for all this, I wonder. Most of his life was spent in tents, overseeing the canal work or digging up fossils. He had a house in Mussoorie (one of the first), but he could not have spent much time in it. It is today part of the Manav Bharti School, and there is still a plaque in the office stating that Cautley lived there. Perhaps he wrote some of his reports and expositions during brief sojourns in the hills. It is said that his wife left him, unable to compete against the rival attractions of canals and fossils remains.

I wonder, too, if there was any follow up on his reports of the submerged city—is it still there, waiting to be re-discovered—or his findings on gold washings in the Siwaliks. Should my royalties ever dry up, I might just wonder off into the Siwaliks, looking for 'gold in them that hills'. Meanwhile, whenever I travel by road from Delhi to Haridwar, and pass over that placid canal at various places en route, I think of the man who spent more than twenty years of his life in executing this magnificent project, and others equally demanding. And then, his work done, walking away from it all without thought of fame or fortune.

A Jungle Princess

From Roorkee, separate roads lead to Haridwar, Saharanpur and Dehradun. And from the Saharanpur road, you can branch off to Paonta Sahib, with its famous gurudwara glistening above the blue waters of the Yamuna. Still blue up here, but not so blue by the time it enters Delhi. Industrial affluents and human waste soon muddy the purest of rivers.

From Paonta you can turn right to Herbertpur, a small township originally settled by an Anglo-Indian family early in the nineteenth century. As may be inferred by its name, Herbert was the scion of the family, but I have been unable to discover much about him. When I was a boy, the Carberry family owned much of the land around here, but by the time Independence came, only one member of the family remained—Doreen, a sultry, dusky beauty who become known in Dehra as the 'Jungle Princess'. Her husband had deserted her, but she had a small daughter who grew up on the land. Doreen's income came from her mango and guava orchards, and she seemed quite happy living in this isolated rural area near the river. Occasionally, she came into Dehradun, a bus ride of a couple of hours, and she would visit my mother, a childhood friend, and occasionally stay overnight.

On one occasion we went to Doreen's jungle home for a couple of days. I was just seven or eight years old. I remember Doreen's daughter (about my age) teaching me to climb trees. I managed the guava tree quite well, but some of the others were too difficult for me.

How did this Jungle Princess manage to live by herself in this remote area, where her house, orchard and fields were bordered by forest on one side and the river on the other?

Well, she had her servants, of course, and they were loyal to her. She also possessed several guns and could handle them very well. I saw her bring down a couple of pheasants with her twelve-bore spread shot. She had also killed a cattle-lifting tiger which had been troubling a nearby village, and a marauding leopard that had taken one of her dogs. So she was quite capable of taking care of herself. When I last saw her, some twenty-five years ago, she was in her seventies. I believe she sold her land and went to live elsewhere with her daughter, who, by then, had a family of her own.

THE BREAK OF MONSOON IN MEERUT

Crossing the Yamuna, still beautiful, before stretches of it came to resemble a huge nullah, the bus took us past a fast-expanding industrial area where a tractor factory was coming up next to a brewery. It was 1962, and I was travelling with my friend Kamal, the two of us having decided to see a bit of Uttar Pradesh. The bus took us across country where General Lake opposed the Maratha forces in 1803 and took Delhi for the British, and over the Hindon river and into UP.

Then north to Meerut, with green fields stretching out on either side: fields of maize, wheat and sugarcane, interspersed with mango orchards and plantations of floating lotus flowers, until we reached the outskirts of the ancient city, got down from the bus, stretched our limbs and climbed onto a cycle rickshaw with our cases and bedding-roll.

The rickshaw boy rode swiftly to the hotel, the only 'English hotel' in Meerut, a building which was probably a barracks at one time, and was owned and managed by a middle-aged Englishman whom we saw, once, when we blundered into the empty building. Apparently, it wasn't a hotel anymore, but Mr P had never bothered to take the signboard down, and if somebody did turn up, as we had done (this only happened about once a year), then they were welcome to a room and the services of his bearer and of course morning tea and breakfast.

Mr P, who lived alone with his wireless, opened a musty room for us and told us to call for the bearer if we needed anything, or wished to pay our bill. During our two-day stay, we never saw him again; he did not emerge from his room, just next to ours; but we heard his radio whenever we cared to listen, mostly relaying BBC cricket commentaries.

Some eighteen miles from Meerut were the remarkable 'Christian' warrior princess Begum Samru's palace and cathedral (she had built both in the very early nineteenth century). We decided to visit them the next day. We took the same rickshaw—the boy attached himself to us for the remainder of our stay—into town on a day so hot and humid that the palace made little impression on me. What does stay in my memory is the restaurant that the rickshaw boy took us to that evening, in the Muslim quarter. It served excellent partridge curry (partridges were plentiful around Meerut) and kebabs. We bought two bottles of beer, which we drank on the verandah back in the hotel, to the crackle and hiss and vaguely military music issuing from Mr P's radio.

Monsoon broke the next day, and my memories of Meerut, ever since, have always been associated with the first rains.

There had been no rain at all for over a month, so the rickshaw boy had told us. Now there were dark clouds overhead, burgeoning with moisture. Thunder blossomed in the air. The dry spell was over. I knew it; the birds knew it; the grass knew it. There was the smell of rain in the air. And the grass, the birds and I responded to this odour with the same sensuous longing. I went out to the balcony and waited.

A large drop of water hit the railing, darkening the thick

dust on the woodwork. A faint breeze had sprung up, and again I felt the moisture, closer and warmer.

Then the rain approached like a dark curtain.

I could see it marching down the street, heavy and remorseless. It drummed on the corrugated tin roof and swept across the road and over the balcony. It swirled with the wind over the trees and roofs of Meerut.

Outside, the street emptied, the crowd dissolved in the rain. Then, buses, cars and bullock carts ploughed through the suddenly rushing water. A garland of marigolds, swept off the steps of a temple, came floating down the middle of the road.

The rain stopped as suddenly as it had begun. The day was dying, and the breeze remained cool and moist. In the brief twilight that followed, I was witness to the great yearly flight of insects into the cool brief freedom of the night.

Termites and white ants, which had been sleeping through the hot season, emerged from their lairs. Out of every hole and crack, and from under the roots of trees, huge winged ants emerged, fluttering about heavily on this, the first and last flight of their lives. There was only one direction in which they could fly—towards the light, towards the street lights and the bright neon tubelight above the balcony.

This was the hour of the geckos, the wall lizards. They had their reward for weeks of patient waiting. Plying their sticky tongues, they crammed their stomachs, knowing that such a feast would not come their way again for a long time. Throughout the long hot season, the insect world had prepared for this flight out of darkness into light, and the phenomenon would not happen again for another year.

Somewhere, an entire orchestra of frogs began their solemn music. The frogs woke great moths out of a slumber and they flew heavily into the balcony. I went in, shut the windows and got into bed thinking of fireflies flashing messages to each other in the mango groves outside Dehra.

FOOTLOOSE IN AGRA

I went to Agra in 1965, to see the Taj. But what interested me about the city had little to do with Emperor Shah Jahan's grand monument to his love.

The cycle rickshaw is the best way of getting about Agra. Its smooth gliding motion and leisurely rate of progress are in keeping with the pace of life in this old-world city. The rickshaw boy makes his way through the crowded bazaars, exchanging insults with tonga drivers, pedestrians and other cyclists; but once on the broad Mall or Taj Road, his curses change to carefree song and he freewheels along the tree-lined avenues. Old colonial-style bungalows still stand in large compounds shaded by peepul, banyan, neem and jamun trees.

Looking up, I notice a number of bright paper kites that flutter, dip and swerve in the cloudless sky. I cannot recall seeing so many kites before.

'Is it a festival today?' I ask,

'No, Sahib,' says the rickshaw boy. 'Not even a holiday.'

'Then why so many kites?'

He does not even bother to look up. 'You can see kites every day, Sahib.'

'I don't see them in Delhi.'

'Ah, but Delhi is a busy place. In Agra, people still fly kites. There are kite-flying competitions every Sunday, and heavy bets are sometimes placed on the outcome.'

As we near the city, I notice kites stuck in trees or dangling from electric wires; but there are always others soaring up to take their place. I ask the rickshaw boy to tell me something about the kite-fliers and the kitemakers, but the subject bores him.

'You had better see the Taj today, Sahib.'

'All right take me to it. I can lunch afterwards.'

It is difficult to view the Taj at noon. The sun strikes the white marble, and there is a great dazzle of reflected light. I stand there with averted eyes, looking at everything—the formal gardens, the surrounding walls of red sandstone, the winding river—everything except the monument I have come to see.

It is there, of course, very solid and real, perfectly preserved, with every jade, jasper or lapis lazuli playing its part in the overall design; and after a while, I can shade my eyes and take in a vision of shimmering white marble. The light rises in waves from the paving-stones, and the squares of black and white marble create an effect of running water. Inside the chamber it is cool and dark but rather musty, and I waste no time in hurrying out again into the sunlight.

I walk the length of a gallery and turn with some relief to the river scene. The sluggish Yamuna winds past Agra on its way to its union with the Ganga. I know the Yamuna well. I know where it emerges from the foothills near Kalsi, cold and blue from the melting snows; I know it as it winds through fields of wheat, sugarcane and mustard, across the flat plains of Uttar Pradesh, sometimes placid, sometimes in flood. I know the river at Delhi, where its muddy banks are a patchwork of clothes spread out by the hundreds of washermen who serve the city and I know it at Mathura, where it is alive with huge turtles; Mathura, sacred city, whose beginnings are lost in antiquity.

And then the river winds its way to Agra, to this spot by the Taj, where parrots flash in the sunshine, kingfishers swoop low over the water and a proud peacock struts across the lawns surrounding the monument.

I follow the peacock into a shady grove. It is quite tame and does not fly away. It leads me to a small boy who is sitting in the shade of a tree, feasting on a handful of small green fruit.

I have not seen the fruit before, and I ask the boy to tell me what it is. He offers me what looks like a hard green plum.

'It is the fruit from the Ashok tree,' says the boy. 'There are many such trees in the garden.'

'Are you allowed to take the fruit?'

'I am allowed,' he says, grinning. 'My father is the head gardener.' I bite into the fruit. It is hard and sour but not unpleasant.

'Do you live here?' I ask.

'Over the wall,' he says. 'But I come here everyday, to help my father and to eat the fruit.'

'So you see the Taj Mahal every day?'

'I have seen it every day for as long as I can remember.'

'And I am seeing it for the first time...you're very lucky.'

He shrugs. 'If you see it once, or a hundred times, it is the same. It doesn't change.'

'Don't you like looking at it, then?'

'I like looking at the people who come here. They are always different. In the evening there will be many people.'

'You must have seen people from almost every country in the world.'

'That is so. They all come here to look at the Taj. Kings and queens and presidents and prime ministers and film stars and poor people too. And I look at them. In that way it isn't boring.'

'Well, you have the Taj to thank for that.'

He gazes thoughtfully at the shimmering monument.

His eyes are accustomed to the sharp sunlight. He sees the Taj every day, but at this moment, he is really looking at it, thinking about it, wondering what magic it must possess to attract people from all corners of the earth, to bring them here, walking through his father's well-kept garden, so that he can have something new and fresh to look at each day.

A cloud—a very small cloud—passes across the face of the sun; and in the softened light I too am able to look at the Taj without screwing up my eyes.

As the boy said, it does not change. Therein lies beauty. For the effect on the traveller is the same today as it was three hundred years ago when Bernier wrote: 'Nothing offends the eye... No part can be found that is not skilfully wrought, or that has not its peculiar beauty.'

And so, for a few moments, this poem in marble is on view to two unimportant people—the itinerant writer and the gardener's boy.

We say nothing; there is really nothing to be said. (But now, a few months later, when I try to recapture the essence of that day, it is not the monument that I remember most vividly. The Taj is there, of course; I still see it as a mirror for the sun. But what remain with me, more than anything else, are the passage of the river and the sharp flavour of the Ashok fruit).

In the afternoon, I walk through the old bazaars which lie to the west of Akbar's great red sandstone fort, and I am not surprised to find a small street which is almost entirely taken up by kite shops. Most of them sell the smaller, cheaper kites, but one small dark shop has in it a variety of odd and fantastic creations. Stepping inside, I find myself face-to-face with the doyen of Agra's kitemakers, Hosain Ali, a feeble old man whose long beard is dyed red with the juice of mehendi leaves. He has just finished making a new kite from bamboo, paper and thin silk, and it lies outside in the sun, firming up. It is a pale pink kite, with a small green tail.

The old man is soon talking to me, for he likes to talk and is not very busy. He complains that few people buy kites these days (I find this hard to believe), and tells me that I should have visited Agra twenty-five years ago, when kite-flying was the sport of kings and even grown men found time to spend an hour or two every day with these dancing strips of paper. Now, he says, everyone hurries, hurries in a heat of hope, and delicate things like kites and daydreams are trampled underfoot. 'Once I made a wonderful kite,' says Hosain Ali nostalgically. 'It was unlike any kite seen in Agra. It had a number of small, very light paper discs trailing on a thin bamboo frame. At the end of each disc I fixed a sprig of grass, forming a balance on both sides. On the first and largest disc I painted a face and gave it eyes made of two small mirrors. The discs, which grew smaller from head to tail, gave the kite the appearance of a crawling serpent. It was very difficult to get this great kite off the ground. Only I could manage it.

'Of course, everyone heard of the Dragon Kite I had made, and word went about that there was some magic in its making. A large crowd arrived on the maidan to watch me fly the kite.

'At first the kite would not leave the ground. The discs made a sharp wailing sound, the sun was trapped in the little mirrors. My kite had eyes and a tongue and a trailing silver tail. I felt it come alive in my hands. It rose from the ground, rose steeply into the sky, moving farther and farther away, with the sun still glinting in its dragon eyes. And when it went very high, it pulled fiercely on the twine, and my son had to help me with the reel.

'But still the kite pulled, determined to be free—yes, it had become a living thing—and at last the twine snapped, and the wind took the kite, took it over the rooftops and the waving trees and the river and the far hills forever. No one ever saw where it fell. Sahib, are you listening? The Dragon Kite is lost, but for you I'll make a bright new poem to fly.'

'Make me one,' I say, moved by his tale, or rather by the manner of its telling. 'I will collect it tomorrow, before I leave Agra. Let it be a beautiful kite. I won't fly it. I'll hang it on my wall, and will not give it a chance to get away.'

It is evening, and the winter sun comes slanting through the intricate branches of a banyan tree, as a cycle rickshaw—a different one this time—brings me to a forgotten corner of Agra that I have always wanted to visit. This is the old Roman Catholic cemetery where so many early European travellers and adventurers lie buried.

Although it is quite probably the oldest Christian cemetery in northern India, it has none of that overgrown, crumbling look that is common to old cemeteries in monsoon lands. It is a bright, even cheerful place, and the jingle of tonga bells and other street noises can be heard from any part of the grounds. The grass is cut, the gravestones are kept clean and most of the inscriptions are still readable.

The caretaker takes me straight to the oldest grave—this is the oldest known European grave in northern India—and it happens to be that of an Englishman, John Mildenhall. The lettering stands out clearly:

Here lies John Mildenhall, Englishman, who left London in 1599 and travelling to India through Persia, reached Agra in 1605 and spoke with the Emperor Akbar. On a second visit in 1614 he fell ill at Lahore, died at Ajmere, and was buried here through the good offices of Thomas Kerridge, Merchant.

During the seventeenth and eighteenth centuries, the Agra cemetery was considered blessed ground by Christians, and the dead were brought here from distant places. Thomas Kerridge must have put himself to considerable expense to bury his friend in Agra. Mildenhall was a romantic, who styled himself an envoy of Queen Elizabeth. Unfortunately, he left no account of his travels, although a couple of his letters are quoted in the writings of Purchas, another English merchant, who lies buried in the Protestant cemetery a couple of furlongs away.

Nearby is the grave of the Venetian, Jerome Veronio, who died at Lahore. According to some old records, he had a hand in designing the Taj, modelling it on Humayun's tomb in Delhi. There had for long been a belief that this 'architect' of the Taj lay buried in the cemetery but no one knew where. Then, in 1945, Father Hyacinth, Superior Regular of Agra, scraped the moss off a tombstone, revealing the simple epitaph: 'Here lies Jerome Veronio, who died at Lahore.'

Actually, there is no evidence that Veronio designed the Taj, and even if he had something to do with it, he was only one of a number of artists and architects who worked on its construction. The chief architect was Muhammed Sharif of Samarkand. Each drew a salary of one thousand rupees per month. Ismail Khan of Turkey was the dome-maker. A number of inlay workers, sculptors and masons were Hindus, including Manohar Singh of

Lahore and Mohan Lal of Kanauj, both famous inlay workers.

A man of more authentic accomplishments was the Italian lapidary, Horten Bronzoni, whose grave lies at a short distance from Veronio's. He died on 11 August 1677. According to Tavernier, it was Bronzoni who cut the Koh-i-noor diamond; and, says Tavernier, he cut the stone very badly.

Bronzoni is again mentioned as having manufactured a model ship of war for Aurangzeb, who had been annoyed by the depredations of Portuguese pirates and was anxious to create a navy. The ship was floated in a huge tank and manoeuvred by a number of European artillerymen. It made a ridiculous sight and convinced the Emperor that a navy was out of the question.

There are over eighty old Armenian graves in the cemetery, but the only one that interests me is the tomb of Shah Azar Khan, an expert in the art of moulding a heavy cannon. One of these, 'Zamzamah', earned a measure of immortality in Kipling's *Kim*—'who holds *Zam-Zammah,* that 'fire-breathing dragon', holds the Punjab, for the great green–bronze piece is always first of the conqueror's loot.' The gun was 14.6 feet long, and is still at Lahore.

Other historic tombs lie scattered about the cemetery, but the most striking and curious of them is the grave of Colonel Jon Hessing, who died in 1803. It is a miniature Taj Mahal, built of red sandstone. Although small compared to a Mughal tomb, it is large for a Christian grave, and could easily accommodate a living family of moderate proportions. Hessing came to India from Holland, and was one of a colourful band of freelance soldiers (most of them deserters) who served in Sindhia's Maratha army. Hessing, we are told, was a good, benevolent man and a great soldier. The tomb was built by his wife Alice, who it must be supposed, felt as tenderly towards the Colonel as Shah

Jahan felt towards his queen. She could not afford marble. Even so, her 'Taj' cost a lakh of rupees.

Outside, in the street, people move about with casual unconcern. Street-vendors occupy the pavement, unwilling that their rivals should take advantage of a brief absence. In the banyan tree, the sparrows and bulbuls are settling down for the night. A kite lies entangled in the upper branches.

ON THE DELHI ROAD

Road travel can involve delays and mishaps, but it also provides you with the freedom to stop where you like and do as you like. I have never found it boring. The seven-hour drive from Mussoorie to Delhi can become a little tiring towards the end, but as I do not drive myself, I can sit back and enjoy everything that the journey has to offer.

I have been to Delhi five times in the last six months—something of a record for me—and on every occasion I have travelled by road. I like looking at the countryside, the passing scene, the people along the road, and this is something I don't see any more from trains; those thick windows of frosted glass effectively cut me off from the world outside.

On my last trip we had to leave the main highway because of a disturbance near Meerut. Instead we had to drive through; about a dozen villages in the prosperous sugarcane belt that dominates this area. It was a wonderful contrast, leaving a main road with its cafes, petrol pumps, factories and management institutes and entering the rural hinterland where very little had changed in a hundred years. Women worked in the fields, old men smoked hookahs in their courtyards, and a few children were playing *guli-danda* instead of cricket! It brought home to me the reality of India—urban life and rural life are still poles apart.

These journeys are seldom without incident. I was sipping a coffee at a wayside restaurant, when a foreign woman walked in, and asked the waiter if they had *à la carte*. Roadside stops seldom provide menus, nor do they go in for French, but our waiter wanted to be helpful, so he led the tourist outside and showed her the way to the public toilet. As she did not return to the restaurant, I have no idea if she eventually found à la carte.

My driver on a recent trip assured me that he knew Delhi very well and could get me to any destination. I told him I'd been booked in a big hotel near the airport, and gave him the name. 'Not to worry', he told me, and drove confidently towards Palam. There, he got confused, and after taking several unfamiliar turnings, drove straight into a large piggery situated behind the airport. We were surrounded by some fifty or sixty pigs and an equal number of children from the mohalla. One boy even asked me if I wanted to purchase a pig. I do like a bit of bacon now and then, but unlike Lord Emsworth, I did not have any ambition to breed prize pigs, so I had to decline. After some arguments over right of way, we were allowed to proceed and finally made it to the hotel.

Occasionally, I have shared a taxi with another passenger, but after one or two disconcerting experiences, I have taken to travelling alone or with a friend.

The last time I shared a taxi with someone, I was pleased to find that my fellow passenger, a large gentleman with a fierce moustache, had bought one of my books, which was lying on the seat between us.

I thought I'd be friendly and so, to break the ice, I remarked 'I see you have one of my books with you,' glancing modestly at the paperback on the seat.

'What do you mean, *your* book?' he bridled, giving me a

dirty look. 'I just bought this book at the news agency!'

'No, no,' I stammered, 'I don't mean it's mine, I mean it's my book—er, that is, I happened to write it!'

'Oh, so now you're claiming to be the author!' He looked at me as though I was a fraud of the worst kind. 'What is your real profession, may I ask?'

'I'm just a typist,' I said, and made no further attempt to make friends.

Indeed, I am very careful about trumpeting my literary or other achievements, as I am frequently misunderstood.

Recently, at a book reading in New Delhi, a little girl asked me how many books I'd written.

'Oh, about sixty or seventy,' I said quite truthfully.

At which another child piped up: 'Why can't you be a little modest about it?'

Sometimes you just can't win.

My author's ego received a salutary beating when on one of my earlier trips, I stopped at a small bookstall and looked around, hoping (like any other author) to spot one of my books. Finally, I found one, under a pile of books by Deepak Chopra, Khushwant Singh, William Dalrymple and other luminaries. I slipped it out from the bottom of the pile and surreptitiously placed it on top.

Unfortunately the bookseller had seen me do this. He picked up the offending volume and returned it to the bottom of the pile, saying 'No demand for this book, sir'.

I wasn't going to tell him I was the author. But just to prove him wrong, I bought the poor neglected thing.

'This is a collector's item,' I told him.

'Ah,' he said, 'At last I meet a collector.'

The number of interesting people I meet on the road is matched only by the number of interesting drivers who have carried me back and forth in their chariots of fire.

The last to do so, the driver of a Qualis, must have had ambitions to be an air pilot. He used the road as a runway and was constantly on the verge of taking off. Pedestrians, cyclists and drivers of smaller vehicles scattered left and right, often hurling abuse at my charioteer, who seemed immune to the most colourful invectives. Trucks did not give way but he simply swerved around them, adopting a zigzag approach to the task of getting from Delhi to Dehradun in the shortest possible time.

'There's no hurry,' I told him more than once, but his English was limited and he told me later that he thought I was saying 'Please hurry!'

Well, he hurried and he harried until at a railway-crossing where we were forced to stop, an irate scooterist came abreast and threatened to turn the driver over to the police. A long and heated argument followed, and it appeared that there would soon be a punch-up, when the crossing-gate suddenly opened and the Qualis flew forward, leaving the fuming scooterist far behind.

As I do not drive myself, I am normally the ideal person to have in the front seat; I repose with complete confidence in the man behind the wheel. And sitting up front, I see more of the road and the passing scene.

One of Mussoorie's better drivers is Sardar Manmohan Singh who drives his own taxi. He is also a keen wildlife enthusiast. It always amazes me how he is able, to drive through the Siwaliks, on a winding hill road, and still keep his eye open for denizens of the surrounding forest.

'See that cheetal!' he would exclaim, or 'What a fine sambhar!' or 'Just look at that elephant!'

All this at high speed. And before I've had time to get more than a fleeting glimpse of one of these creatures, we would be well past them.

Manmohan swears that he has seen a tiger crossing the road near the Mohand Pass, and as he is a person of some integrity, I have to believe him. I think the tiger appears especially for Manmohan.

Another wildlife enthusiast is my old friend Vishal Ohri, of State Bank fame. On one occasion he drove me down a forest road between Haridwar and Mohand, and we did indeed see a number of animals, including cheetal and wild boar.

Unlike our car drivers, he was in no hurry to reach our destination and would stop every now and then, in order to examine the footprints of elephants. He also pointed out large dollops of fresh elephant dung, proof that wild elephants were in the vicinity. I did not think his old Fiat would outrun an angry elephant and urged him to get a move on before nightfall. Vishal then held forth on the benefits of elephant dung and how it could be used to reinforce mud walls. I assured him that I would try it out on the walls of my study, which was in danger of falling down.

Vishal was well ahead of his time. Only the other day I read in one of our papers that elephant dung. could be converted into good quality paper. Perhaps they'll use it to make bank notes. Reserve Bank, please note.

◆

Other good drivers who have taken me here and there include Ganesh Saili, who who is even better after a few drinks;

Victor Banerjee who is better before drinks; and young Harpreet who is a fan of Kenny G's saxophone playing. On the road to Delhi with Harpreet, I had six hours of listening to Kenny G on tape. On my return, two days later, I had another six hours of Kenny G. Now I go into a frenzy whenever I hear a saxophone.

My publisher has an experienced old driver who also happens to be quite deaf. He blares the car horn vigorously and without respite. When I asked him why he used the horn so much, he replied, "Well, I can't hear *their* horns, but I'll make sure they hear mine!' As good a reason as any.

It is sometimes said that women don't make good drivers, but I beg to differ. Mrs Biswas was an excellent driver but a dangerous woman to know. Her husband had been a well-known shikari, and he kept a stuffed panther in the drawing room of his Delhi farm-house. Mrs Biswas spent the occasional weekend at her summer home in Landour. I'd been to one or two of her parties, attended mostly by menfolk.

One day, while I was loitering on the road, she drove up and asked me if I'd like to accompany her down to Dehradun.

'I'll come with you,' I said, 'provided we can have a nice lunch at Kwality.'

So, down the hill we glided, and Mrs Biswas did some shopping, and we lunched at Kwality, and got back into her car and set off again—but in a direction opposite to Mussoorie and Landour.

Where are we going?' I asked.

'To Delhi, of course. Aren't you coming with me?'

I didn't know we were going to Delhi. I didn't even have my pyjamas with me.

'Don't worry,' said Mrs B. 'My husband's pyjamas will fit you.

'He may not want me to wear his pyjamas,' I protested.
'Oh, don't worry. He's in London just now.'

I persuaded Mrs Biswas to stop at the nearest bus stop, bid her farewell and took the bus back to Mussoorie. She may have been a good driver but I had no intention of ending up stuffed alongside the stuffed panther in the drawing room.

SACRED SHRINES ALONG THE WAY

Nandprayag: Where Rivers Meet

It's a funny thing, but long before I arrive at a place I can usually tell whether I am going to like it or not.

Thus, while I was still some twenty miles from the town of Pauri, I felt it was not going to be my sort of place; and sure enough, it wasn't. On the other hand, while Nandprayag was still out of sight, I knew I was going to like it. And I did. Perhaps it's something on the wind-emanations of an atmosphere that are carried to me well before I arrive at my destination. I can't really explain it, and no doubt it is silly to make judgements in advance. But it happens and I mention the fact for what it's worth.

As for Nandprayag, perhaps I'd been there in some previous existence, I felt I was nearing home as soon as we drove into this cheerful roadside hamlet, some little way above the Nandakini's confluence with the Alakananda river. A prayag is a meeting place of two rivers, and as there are many rivers in the Garhwal Himalayas, all linking up to join either the Ganga or the Yamuna, it follows that there are numerous prayags, in themselves places of pilgrimage as well as wayside halts enroute to the higher Hindu shrines at Kedarnath and Badrinath. Nowhere else in the Himalayas are there so many temples, sacred streams, holy places and holy men.

Some little way above Nandprayag's busy little bazaar, is the tourist rest house, perhaps the nicest of the tourist lodges in this region. It has a well-kept garden surrounded by fruit trees and is a little distance from the general hubbub of the main road.

Above it is the old pilgrim path, on which you walked. Just a few decades ago, if you were a pilgrim intent on finding salvation at the abode of the gods, you travelled on foot all the way from the plains, covering about 200 miles in a couple of months. In those days people had the time, the faith and the endurance. Illness and misadventure often dogged their footsteps, but what was a little suffering if at the end of the day they arrived at the very portals of heaven? Some did not survive to make the return journey. Today's pilgrims may not be lacking in devotion, but most of them do expect to come home again.

Along the pilgrim path are several handsome old houses, set among mango trees and the fronds of papaya and banana. Higher up the hill, the pine forests commence, but down here it is almost subtropical. Nandprayag is only about 3,000 feet above sea level—a height at which the vegetation is usually quite lush, provided there is protection from the wind.

In one of these double-storeyed houses lives Mr Devki Nandan, scholar and recluse. He welcomes me into his house and plies me with food till I am close to bursting. He has a great love for his little corner of Garhwal and proudly shows me his collection of clippings concerning this area. One of them is from a travelogue by Sister Nivedita—an Englishwoman, Margaret Noble, who became an interpreter of Hinduism to the West. Visiting Nandprayag in 1928, she wrote:

> Nandprayag is a place that ought to be famous for its beauty and order. For a mile or two before reaching it

we had noticed the superior character of the agriculture and even some careful gardening of fruits and vegetables. The peasantry also, suddenly grew handsome, not unlike the Kashmiris. The town itself is new, rebuilt since the Gohna flood, and its temple stands far out across the fields on the shore of the Prayag. But in this short time a wonderful energy has been at work on architectural carvings, and the little place is full of gemlike beauties. Its temple is dedicated to Naga Takshaka. As the road crosses the river, I noticed two or three old Pathan tombs, the only traces of Mohammedanism that we had seen north of Srinagar in Garhwal.

Little has changed since Sister Nivedita's visit, and there is still a small and thriving Pathan population in Nandprayag. In fact, when I called on Mr Nandan, he was in the act of sending out Eid greetings to his Muslim friends. Some of the old graves have disappeared in the debris from new road cuttings: an endless business, this road-building. And as for the beautiful temple described by Sister Nivedita, I was sad to learn that it had been swept away by a mighty flood in 1970, when a cloudburst and subsequent landslide on the Alakananda resulted in great destruction downstream.

Mr Nandan remembers the time when he walked to the small hill station of Pauri to join the old Messmore Mission School, where so many famous sons of Garhwal received their early education. It would take him four days to get to Pauri. Now it is just four hours by bus. It was only after the Chinese invasion of 1962 that there was a rush of road-building in the hill districts of northern India. Before that, everyone walked and thought nothing of it!

Sitting alone that same evening in the little garden of the rest house, I heard innumerable birds break into song. I did not see any of them, because the light was fading and the trees were dark, but there was the rather melancholy call of the hill dove, the insistent ascending trill of the koel, and much shrieking, whistling and twittering that I was unable to assign to any particular species.

Now, once again, while I sit on the lawn surrounded by zinnias in full bloom, I am teased by that feeling of having been here before, on this lush hillside, among the pomegranates and oleanders. Is it some childhood memory asserting itself? But as a child I had never travelled in these parts.

True, Nandprayag had some affinity with parts of the Doon Valley before it was submerged by a tidal wave of humanity. But in the Doon there is no great river running past your garden. Here there are two, and they are also part of this feeling of belonging. Perhaps in some former life I did come this way, or maybe I dreamed about living here. Who knows? Anyway, mysteries are more interesting than certainties. Presently the room-boy joins me for a chat on the lawn. He is, in fact, running the rest house in the absence of the manager. A coachload of pilgrims is due at any moment but until they arrive, the place is empty and only the birds can be heard. His name is Janakpal and he tells me something about his village on the next mountain, where a leopard has been carrying off goats and cattle. He doesn't think much of the conservationists' law protecting leopards: nothing can be done unless the animal becomes a man-eater!

A shower of rain descends on us, and so do the pilgrims. Janakpal leaves me to attend to his duties. But I am not left alone for long. A youngster with a cup of tea appears. He wants me to take him to Mussoorie or Delhi. He is fed up, he says, with washing dishes here.

'You are better off here,' I tell him sincerely. 'In Mussoorie, you will have twice as many dishes to wash. In Delhi, ten times as many.'

'Yes, but there are cinemas there,' he says, 'and television, and videos.' I am left without an argument. Birdsong may have charms for me but not for the restless dishwasher in Nandprayag.

The rain stops and I go for a walk. The pilgrims keep to themselves but the locals are always ready to talk. I remember a saying (and it may have originated in these hills), which goes: 'All men are my friends. I have only to meet them.' In these hills, where life still moves at a leisurely and civilized pace, one is constantly meeting them.

The Magic of Tungnath

The mountains and valleys of Uttaranchal never fail to spring surprises on the traveller in search of the picturesque. It is impossible to know every corner of the Himalayas, which means that there are always new corners to discover; forest or meadow, mountain stream or wayside shrine.

The temple of Tungnath, at a little over 12,000 feet, is the highest shrine on the inner Himalayan range. It lies just below the Chandrashila peak. Some way off the main pilgrim routes, it is less frequented than Kedarnath or Badrinath, although it forms a part of the Kedar temple establishment. The priest here is a local man, a Brahmin from the village of Maku; the other Kedar temples have South Indian priests, a tradition begun by Sankaracharya, the eighth century Hindu reformer and revivalist.

Tungnath's lonely eminence gives it a magic of its own. To

get there (or beyond), one passes through some of the most delightful temperate forests in the Garhwal Himalayas. Pilgrim, or trekker, or just plain rambler such as myself, one comes away a better person, forest-refreshed, and more aware of what the world was really like before mankind began to strip it bare.

Duiri Tal, a small lake, lies cradled on the hill above Okhimath, at a height of 8,000 feet. It was a favourite spot of one of Garhwal's earliest British Commissioners, J.H. Batten, whose administration continued for twenty years (1836–56). He wrote:

> The day I reached there, it was snowing and young trees were laid prostrate under the weight of snow; the lake was frozen over to a depth of about two inches. There was no human habitation, and the place looked a veritable wilderness. The next morning when the sun appeared, the Chaukhamba and many other peaks extending as far as Kedarnath seemed covered with a new quilt of snow, as if close at hand. The whole scene was so exquisite that one could not tire of gazing at it for hours. I think a person who has a subdued settled despair in his mind would all of a sudden feel a kind of bounding and exalting cheerfulness which will be imparted to his frame by the atmosphere of Duiri Tal.

This feeling of upliftment can be experienced almost anywhere along the Tungnath range. Duiri Tal is still some way off the beaten track, and anyone wishing to spend the night there should carry a tent; but further along this range, the road ascends to Dugalbeta (at about 9,000 feet) where a PWD rest house, gaily painted, has come up like some exotic orchid in the midst of a lush meadow topped by excelsia pines and pencil cedars.

Many an official who has stayed here has rhapsodized on the charms of Dugalbeta; and if you are unofficial (and therefore not entitled to stay in the bungalow), you can move on to Chopta, lusher still, where there is accommodation of a sort for pilgrims and other hardy souls. Two or three little tea shops provide mattresses and quilts. The Garhwal Mandal is putting up a rest house. These tourist rest houses of Garhwal are a great boon to the traveller; but during the pilgrim season (May/June), they are filled to the point of overflowing, and if you turn up unexpectedly, you might have to take your pick of tea-shop or 'dharamshala': something of a lucky dip, since they vary a good deal in comfort and cleanliness.

The trek from Chopta to Tungnath is only three and a half miles, but in that distance one ascends about 3,000 feet, and the pilgrim may be forgiven for feeling that at places he is on a perpendicular path. Like a ladder to heaven, I couldn't help thinking.

In spite of its steepness, my companion, the redoubtable Ganesh Saili, insisted that we take a shortcut. After clawing our way up tufts of alpine grass, which formed the rungs of our ladder, we were stuck and had to inch our way down again; so that the ascent of Tungnath began to resemble a game of Snakes and Ladders.

A tiny guardian-temple dedicated to the god Ganesh spurred us on. Nor was I really fatigued; for the cold fresh air and the verdant greenery surrounding us was like an intoxicant. Myriad wildflowers grow on the open slopes—buttercups, anemones, wild strawberries, forget-me-not, rock-cress—enough to rival Bhyundar's 'Valley of Flowers' at this time of the year.

But before reaching these alpine meadows, we climb through rhododendron forest, and here one finds at least three species of this flower: the red-flowering tree rhododendron (found throughout the Himalayas between 6,000 feet and 10,000 feet); a second variety, the almatta, with flowers that are light red or rosy in colour; and the third chimul or white variety, found at heights ranging from between 10,000 and 13,000 feet. The chimul is a brush-wood, seldom more than twelve feet high and growing slantingly due to the heavy burden of snow it has to carry for almost six months in the year.

These brushwood rhododendrons are the last trees we see on our ascent, for as we approach Tungnath the tree line ends and there is nothing between earth and sky except grass and rock and tiny flowers. Above us, a couple of crows dive-bomb a hawk, who does his best to escape their attentions. Crows are the world's great survivors. They are capable of living at any height and in any climate; as much at home in the back streets of Delhi as on the heights of Tungnath.

Another survivor up here at any rate, is the pika, a sort of mouse-hare, who looks like neither mouse nor hare but rather a tiny guinea-pig—small ears, no tail, grey-brown fur, and chubby feet. They emerge from their holes under the rocks to forage for grasses on which to feed. Their simple diet and thick fur enable them to live in extreme cold, and they have been found at 16,000 feet, which is higher than where any other mammal lives. The Garhwalis call this little creature the 'runda'—at any rate, that's what the temple priest called it, adding that it was not averse to entering houses and helping itself to grain and other delicacies. So perhaps there's more in it of mouse than of hare.

These little rundas were with us all the way from Chopta to Tungnath; peering out from their rocks or scampering about on the hillside, seemingly unconcerned by our presence. At

Tungnath they live beneath the temple flagstones. The priest's grandchildren were having a game discovering their burrows; the rundas would go in at one hole and pop out at another—they must have had a system of underground passages.

When we arrived, clouds had gathered over Tungnath as they do almost every afternoon. The temple looked austere in the gathering gloom.

To some, the name 'tung' indicates 'lofty', from the position of the temple on the highest peak outside the main chain of the Himalayas; others derive it from the word 'tunga', that is 'to be suspended'—an allusion to the form under which the deity is worshipped here. The form is the Swayambhu Ling. On Shivratri or the Night of Shiva, the true believer may, 'with the eye of faith', see the lingam increase in size; but 'to the evil-minded no such favour is granted.'

The temple, though not very large, is certainly impressive, mainly because of its setting and the solid slabs of grey granite from which it is built. The whole place somehow puts me in mind of Emily Brontë's *Wuthering Heights*—bleak, windswept, open to the skies. And as you look down from the temple at the little half-deserted hamlet that serves it in summer, the eye is met by grey slate roofs and piles of stones, with just a few hardy souls in residence—for the majority of pilgrims now prefer to spend the night down at Chopta.

Even the temple priest, attended by his son and grandsons, complains bitterly of the cold. To spend every day barefoot on those cold flagstones must indeed be hardship. I wince after five minutes of it, made worse by stepping into a puddle of icy water. I shall never make a good pilgrim; no rewards for me, in this world or the next. But the pandit's feet are literally thick-skinned; and the children seem oblivious to the cold. Still in

October, they must be happy to descend to Maku, their home village on the slopes below Dugalbeta.

It begins to rain as we leave the temple. We pass herds of sheep huddled in a ruined dharamshala. The crows are still rushing about the grey, weeping skies, although the hawk has very sensibly gone away. A runda sticks his nose out from his hole, probably to take a look at the weather. There is a clap of thunder and he disappears, like the white rabbit in *Alice in Wonderland*. We are halfway down the Tungnath 'ladder' when it begins to rain quite heavily. And now we pass our first genuine pilgrims, a group of intrepid Bengalis who are heading straight into the storm. They are without umbrellas or raincoats, but they are not to be deterred. Oaks and rhododendrons flash past as we dash down the steep, winding path. Another shortcut, and Ganesh Saili takes a tumble, but is cushioned by moss and buttercups. My wristwatch strikes a rock and the glass is shattered. No matter. Time here is of little or no consequence. Away with time! Is this, I wonder, the 'bounding and exalting cheerfulness' experienced by Batten and now manifesting itself in me?

The tea-shop beckons. How would one manage in the hills without these wayside tea shops? Miniature inns, they provide food, shelter and even lodging to dozens at a time. We sit on a bench between a Gujjar herdsman and a pilgrim who is too feverish to make the climb to the temple. He accepts my offer of an aspirin to go with his tea. We tackle some buns-rock-hard, to match our environment—and wash the pellets down with hot sweet tea.

There is a small shrine here too, right in front of the tea-shop. It is a slab of rock roughly shaped like a lingam, and it is daubed with vermilion and strewn with offerings of wildflowers. The mica in the rock gives it a beautiful sheen.

I suppose Hinduism comes closest to being a nature religion. Rivers, rocks, trees, plants, animals and birds, all play their part, both in mythology and in everyday worship. This harmony is most evident in these remote places, where gods and mountains coexist. Tungnath, as yet unspoilt by a materialistic society, exerts its magic on all who come here with open mind and heart.

BREAKFAST TIME

I like a good sausage, I do;
It's a dish for the chosen and few.
Oh, for sausage and mash,
And of mustard a dash,
And an egg nicely fried—maybe two?
At breakfast or lunch, or at dinner,
The sausage is always a winner;
If you want a good spread,
Go for sausage on bread,
And forget all your vows to be slimmer.

'In Praise of the Sausage'
(Written for Victor and Maya Banerjee,
who excel at making sausage breakfasts.)

There is something to be said for breakfast.

If you take an early morning walk down Landour Bazaar, you might be fortunate enough to see a very large cow standing in the foyer of a hotel, munching on a succulent cabbage or cauliflower. The owner of the hotel has a soft spot for this particular cow, and invites it in for breakfast every morning. Having had its fill, the cow—very well-behaved—backs out of the shop and makes way for paying customers.

I am not one of them. I prefer to have my breakfast at home—a fried egg, two or three buttered toasts, a bit of bacon if I'm lucky, otherwise some fish pickle from the south, followed by a cup of strong coffee—and I'm a happy man and can take the rest of the day in my stride.

I don't think I have ever written a good story without a good breakfast. There are, of course, writers who do not eat before noon. Both they and their prose have a lean and hungry look. Dickens was good at describing breakfasts and dinners—especially Christmas repasts—and many of his most rounded characters were good-natured people who were fond of their food and drink—Mr Pickwick, the Cheeryble brothers, Mr Weller senior, Captain Cuttle—as opposed to the half-starved characters in the works of some other Victorian writers. And remember, Dickens had an impoverished childhood. So I took it as a compliment when a little girl came up to me the other day and said, 'Sir, you're Mr Pickwick!'

As a young man, I had a lean and hungry look. After all, I was often hungry. Now if I look like Pickwick, I take it as an achievement.

And all those breakfasts had something to do with it.

It's not only cows and early-to-rise writers who enjoy a good breakfast. Last summer, Colonel Solomon was out taking his pet Labrador for an early morning walk near Lal Tibba when a leopard sprang out of a thicket, seized the dog and made off with it down the hillside. The dog did not even have time to yelp. Nor did the Colonel. Suffering from shock, he left Landour the next day and has yet to return.

Another leopard—this time at the other end of Mussoorie—entered the Savoy hotel at dawn, and finding nothing in the kitchen except chicken's feathers, moved on to the billiard room and there vented its frustration on the cloth of the billiard table, clawing it to shreds. The leopard was seen in various parts of the hotel before it made off in the direction of the Ladies' Block.

Just a hungry leopard in search of a meal. But three days later, Nandu Jauhar, the owner of the Savoy, found himself short of a lady housekeeper. Had she eloped with the laundryman, or had she become a good breakfast for the leopard? We do not know till this day.

English breakfasts, unlike continental breakfasts, are best enjoyed in India where you don't have to rush off to catch a bus or a train or get to your office in time. You can linger over your scrambled egg and marmalade on toast. What would breakfast be without some honey or marmalade? You can have an excellent English breakfast at the India International Centre, where I have spent many pleasant reflective mornings... And a super breakfast at the Raj Mahal Hotel in Jaipur. But some hotels give very inferior breakfasts, and I am afraid that certain Mussoorie establishments are great offenders, specializing in singed omelettes and burnt toasts.

Many people are under the erroneous impression that the days of the British Raj were synonymous with huge meals and unlimited food and drink. This may have been the case in the days of the East India Company, but was far from being so during the last decade of British rule. Those final years coincided with World War II, when food rationing was in force. At my boarding school in Shimla, omelettes were made from powdered eggs, and the contents of the occasional sausage were very mysterious—so much so, that we called our sausages 'sweet mysteries of life!' after a popular Nelson Eddy song.

Things were not much better at home. Just porridge (no eggs!) bread and jam (no butter!), and tea with *ghur* instead of refined sugar. The *ghur* was, of course, much healthier than sugar.

Breakfasts are better now, at least for those who can afford them. The jam is better than it used to be. So is the bread. And I can enjoy a fried egg, or even two, without feeling guilty about it. But good omelettes are still hard to come by. They shouldn't be made in a hurried or slapdash manner. Some thought has to go into an omelette. And a little love too. It's like writing a book—done much better with some feeling!

THE OPEN ROAD

As the years go by, I do not walk as far or as fast as I used to; but speed and distance were never my forte. Like J. Krishnamurti, I believe that the journey is more important than the destination. But, then, I have never really had a destination. The glory that comes from conquering the Himalayan peaks is not for me. My greatest pleasure lies in taking a path—any old path will do—and following it until it leads me to a forest glade or village or stream or windy hilltop.

This sort of tramping (it does not even qualify as trekking) is a compulsive thing with me. You could call it my vice, since it is stronger than the desire for wine, women or song. To get on to the open road fills me with joie de vivre, gives me an exhilaration not found in other, possibly more worthy, pursuits.

Only this afternoon I had one of my more enjoyable tramps. I had been cooped up in my room for several days, while outside it rained and hailed and snowed and the wind blew icily from all directions. It seemed ages since I'd taken a long walk. Fed up with it all, I pulled on my overcoat, banged the door shut and set off up the hillside.

I kept to the main road, but because of the heavy snow, there were no vehicles on it. Even as I walked, flurries of snow struck my face, and collected on my coat and head. Up at the top of the hill, the deodars were clothed in a mantle of white.

It was fairyland: everything still and silent. The only movement was the circling of an eagle over the trees. I walked for an hour, and passed only one person, the milkman on his way back to his village. His cans were crowned with snow. He looked a little tipsy. He asked me the time, but before I could tell him, he shook me by the hand and said I was a good fellow because I never complained about the water in the milk. I told him that as long as he used clean water, I'd contain my wrath.

On my way back, I passed a small group. It consisted of a person in some sort of uniform (because of the snow I couldn't really make it out), who was hurling epithets at several small children who were busy throwing snowballs at him. He kept shouting: 'Do you know who I am? Do you know who I am?' The children did not want to know. They were only interested in hitting their target, and succeeded once in every five or six attempts.

I came home exhilarated and immediately sat down beside the stove to write this piece. I found some lines of Stevenson's which seemed appropriate:

> *And this shall be for music when no one else is near,*
> *The fine song for singing, the rare song to hear!*
> *That only I remember, that only you admire,*
> *Of the broad road that stretches, and the roadside fire.*

He speaks directly to me, across the mists of time: R.L. Stevenson, prince of essayists. There is none like him today. We hurry, hurry in a heat of hope—and who has time for roadside fires, except, perhaps, those who must work on the roads in all weathers?

Whenever I walk into the hills, I come across gangs of road workers breaking stones, cutting into the rocky hillsides, building retaining walls. I am not against more roads—especially in the hills, where the people have remained impoverished largely because of the inaccessibility of their villages. Besides, a new road is one more road for me to explore, and in the interests of progress, I am prepared to put up with the dust raised by the occasional bus. And if it becomes too dusty, one can always leave the main road. There is no dearth of paths leading off into the valleys.

On one such diversionary walk, I reached a village where I was given a drink of curd and a meal of rice and beans. That is another of the attractions of tramping to nowhere in particular—the finding of somewhere in particular; the striking up of friendships; the discovery of new springs and waterfalls, unusual plants, rare flowers, strange birds. In the hills, a new vista opens up at every bend in the road. That is what makes me a compulsive walker—new vistas, and the charm of the unexpected.

ALL ABOUT MY WALKABOUTS

All my life I've been a walking person. Up to this day, I have neither owned nor driven a car, bus, tractor, airplane, motorcycle, truck or steamroller. Forced to make a choice, I would as soon drive a steamroller, because of its slow but solid progress and unhurried finality. And also because other vehicles don't try hustling steamrollers off the road.

For a brief period in my early teens I had a bicycle, until I rode into a bullock cart and ruined my new cycle. The bullocks panicked and ran away with the cart while the furious cart driver was giving me a lecture on road sense. I have never bumped into a bullock cart while walking.

My earliest memories are of a place called Jamnagar, a small port on the west coast of India, then part of a princely state. My father was an English tutor to several young Indian princes and princesses. This was where my walking really began because Jamnagar was full of spacious palaces, lawns and gardens. By the time I was four, I was exploring much of this territory on my own, with the result that I encountered my first snake. Instead of striking me dead as snakes are supposed to do, it allowed me to pass.

Living as it did so close to the ground, and sensitive to every footfall, it must have known instinctively that I presented no threat, that I was just another small creature discovering the use of his legs. Envious of the snake's swift gliding movements, I went indoors and tried crawling about on my belly. But I wasn't much good at it. Legs were better.

My father's schoolroom and our own residence were located on the grounds of one of the older palaces, which was full of turrets stairways and mysterious dark passages. Right on top of the building, I discovered a glass-covered room, each pane of glass stained with a different colour. This room fascinated me as I could, by turn, look through the panes of glass at a green or rose-pink or orange or deep indigo world. It was nice to be able to decide for oneself what colour the world should be!

My father took his duties seriously and taught me to read and write long before I started attending a regular school. However, it would be true to say that I first learned to read upside down. This happened because I would sit on a stool in front of the three princesses, watching them read and write, and so the view I had of their books was an upside down view. I still read that way occasionally, especially when a book becomes boring.

There was no boredom in the palace grounds. We were situated in the middle of a veritable jungle of a garden, where marigolds and cosmos grew rampantly in the long grass. An old disused well was the home of countless pigeons, their gentle cooing by day contrasting with the shrill cries of the brainfever bird (the hawk-cuckoo) at night. 'How very hot it's getting!' the bird seems to say. And then, in a rising crescendo, 'We feel it! *We feel it!* WE FEEL IT!

Walking along a nearby beach, collecting seashells, I got into the habit of staring hard at the ground, a habit which has remained with me all my life. Apart from helping my thought processes, it also results in my picking up odd objects—coins, keys, broken bangles, marbles, pens, bits of crockery, pretty stones, feathers, ladybirds, seashells, snail shells, not to speak of old nails and horseshoes.

Looking at my collection of miscellaneous objects picked up on these walks, my friends insist that I must be using a metal detector. But it's only because I keep my nose to the ground like a bloodhound.

Occasionally, of course, this habit results in my walking some way past my destination (if I happen to have one). And why not? It simply means discovering a new and different destination, sights and sounds that I might not have experienced had I ended my walk exactly where it was supposed to end. And I am not looking at the ground all the time. Sensitive like a snake to approaching footfalls, I look up from time to time to take note of the faces of passers-by, just in case they have something interesting to say.

A bird singing in a bush or tree has my immediate attention, so does any familiar flower or plant, particularly if it grows in an unusual place such as a crack in a wall or rooftop, or in a yard full of junk—where once I found a rosebush blooming on the roof of an old, abandoned Ford car.

I like to think that I invented the zigzag walk. Tiring of walking in straight lines, or on roads that led directly to a destination, I took to going off at tangents—taking sudden unfamiliar turnings, wandering down narrow alleyways, following cart tracks or paths through fields instead of the main roads, and in general making the walk as complicated as possible.

In this way, I saw much more than I would normally have seen. Here a temple, there a mosque; now an old church; a railway siding; follow the railway line; here's a pond full of buffaloes, there a peacock preening itself under a tamarind tree; and now I'm in a field of mustard, and soon I'm walking along a canal bank, and the canal leads me back into the town, and I follow the line of the mango trees until I am home.

The adventure is not in arriving, it's the on-the-way experience. It is not the expected; it's the surprise. You are not choosing what you shall see in the world, but are giving the world an even chance to see you.

It's like drawing lines from star to star in the night sky, not forgetting many dim, shy, out-of-the-way stars, which are full of possibilities. The first turning to the left, the next to the right! I am still on my zigzag way, pursuing the diagonal between reason and heart.

PICNIC AT FOX BURN

In spite of the frenetic building activity in most hill stations, there are still a few ruins to be found on the outskirts—neglected old bungalows that have fallen or been pulled down, and which now provide shelter for bats, owls, stray goats, itinerant sadhus and sometimes the restless spirits of those who once dwelt in them.

One such ruin is Fox Burn, but I won't tell you exactly where it can be found because I visit the place for purposes of meditation (or just plain contemplation), and I would hate to arrive there one morning to find about fifty people picnicking on the grass.

And yet it did witness a picnic of sorts the other day, when the children accompanied me to the ruin. They had heard it was haunted, and they wanted to see the ghost.

Rakesh is twelve, Mukesh is six and Dolly is four, and they are not afraid of ghosts.

I should mention here, that before Fox Burn became a ruin, back in the 1940s, it was owned by an elderly Englishwoman, Mrs Williams, who ran it as a boarding house for several years. In the end, poor health forced her to give up this work, and during her last years, she lived alone in the huge house, with just a chowkidar to help. Her children, who had grown up on the property, had long since settled in faraway lands.

When Mrs Williams died, the chowkidar stayed on for some time until the property was disposed of; but he left as soon as he could. Late at night, there would be a loud rapping on his door, and he would hear the old lady calling out: 'Shamsher Singh, open the door! Open the door, I say, and let me in!'

Needless to say, Shamsher Singh kept the door firmly closed. He returned to his village at the first opportunity. The hill-station was going through a slump at the time, and the new owners pulled the house down and sold the roof and beams as scrap.

'What does Fox Burn mean?' asked Rakesh, as we climbed the neglected, overgrown path to the ruin.

'Well, Burn is a Scottish word meaning stream or spring. Perhaps there was a spring here, once. If so, it dried up long ago.'

'And did a fox live here?'

'Maybe a fox came to drink at the spring. There are still foxes living on the mountain. Sometimes you can see them dancing in the moonlight.'

Passing through a gap in a wall, we came upon the ruins of the house. In the bright light of a summer morning, it did not look in the least spooky or depressing. A line of Doric pillars were all that remained of what must have been an elegant porch and verandah. Beyond them, through the deodars, we could see the distant snows. It must have been a lovely spot in which to spend the better part of one's life. No wonder Mrs Williams wanted to come back.

The children were soon scampering about on the grass, whilst I sought shelter beneath a huge chestnut tree. There is no tree so friendly as the chestnut, especially in summer when it is in full leaf.

Mukesh discovered an empty water tank and Rakesh

suggested that it had once fed the burn that no longer existed. Dolly busied herself making nosegays with the daisies that grew wild in the grass.

Rakesh looked up suddenly. He pointed to a path on the other side of the ruin, and exclaimed: 'Look, what's that? Is it Mrs Williams?'

'A ghost!' said Mukesh excitedly.

But it turned out to be the local washerwoman, a large white bundle on her head, taking a shortcut across the property.

A more peaceful place could hardly be imagined, until a large black dog, a spaniel of sorts, arrived on the scene. He wanted someone to play with—indeed, he insisted on playing—and ran circles round us until we threw sticks for him to fetch and gave him half our sandwiches.

'Whose dog is it?' asked Rakesh.

'I've no idea.'

'Did Mrs Williams keep a black dog?'

'Is it a ghost dog?' asked Mukesh.

'It looks real to me,' I said.

'And it has eaten all my biscuits,' said Dolly.

'Don't ghosts have to eat?' asked Mukesh.

'I don't know. We'll have to ask one.'

'It can't be any fun being a ghost if you can't eat,' declared Mukesh.

The black dog left us as suddenly as he had appeared, and as there was no sign of an owner, I began to wonder if he had not, after all, been an apparition.

A cloud came over the sun, the air grew chilly.

'Let's go home,' said Mukesh.

'I'm hungry,' said Rakesh.

'Come along, Dolly,' I called.

But Dolly couldn't be seen.

We called out to her, and looked behind trees and pillars, certain that she was hiding from us. Almost five minutes passed in searching for her, and a sick feeling of apprehension was coming over me, when Dolly emerged from the ruins and ran towards us.

'Where have you been?' we demanded, almost with one voice.

'I was playing—in there—in the old house. Hide and seek.'

'On your own?'

'No, there were two children. A boy and a girl. They were playing too.'

'I haven't seen any children,' I said.

'They've gone now.'

'Well, it's time we went too.'

We set off down the winding path, with Rakesh leading the way, and then we had to wait because Dolly had stopped and was waving to someone.

'Who are you waving to, Dolly?'

'To the children.'

'Where are they?'

'Under the chestnut tree.'

'I can't see them. Can you see them, Rakesh? Can you, Mukesh?'

Rakesh and Mukesh said they couldn't see any children. But Dolly was still waving.

'Goodbye,' she called. 'Goodbye!'

Were there voices on the wind? Faint voices calling goodbye?

Could Dolly see something we couldn't see?

'We can't see anyone,' I said.

'No,' said Dolly. 'But they can see me!'

Then she left off her game and joined us, and we ran home

laughing. Mrs Williams may not have revisited her old house that day but perhaps her children had been there, playing under the chestnut tree they had known so long ago.

THE ROAD TO ANJANI SAIN

Fog, mist, cloud, rain and mildew—these were the things the British must have looked for when selecting suitable sites for the hill stations they set up in the Himalayan foothills 150 years ago: Shimla, Mussoorie, Darjeeling, Dalhousie, Nainital, all soggy with monsoon or winter mist and dripping oaks and deodars. The climate must have reminded them of their homes on the English moors or the Scottish highlands.

I have survived all that through the forty or so mountain monsoons that have been thrown at me; and having gone through the annual ritual of wiping the mildew from my books and a certain green fungus from my one and only suit, I decided some years ago to leave cloud country behind for a few days and be the guest of Cyril Raphael, at the Bhuvneshwari Mahila Ashram (a social service organization), at Anjani Sain in Tehri-Garhwal.

Pine country this, dry and bracing, with the scent of pine resin in the air. I have always thought 5,000 to 6,000 feet a healthier altitude to live at, but perhaps I'm prejudiced, having been born in Kasauli, which is pine rather than deodar country. Anjani Sain is about the same height and gets the sun all day. Given adequate food and pure water, it's a healthy place to live. Contrary to what most people think, Garhwal is not a poverty-stricken area. Almost everyone has a bit of land and does at least have the traditional do roti for sustenance, which is more than can be said for the urban unemployed in other parts of northern India. But medical facilities are certainly lacking.

This area has always been known as Khas-patti, probably because it was special in several ways—climate-wise and probably economy-wise too. Down in the flat valley, there are green fields and even mango trees, the descent to lower altitudes being quite sudden in these parts. The small Anjani Sain bazaar, with its single bank, post office and chemist's shop, shimmers in the noon sun; it looks like a set for a gunfight like in old westerns. But this is, generally, a peaceful area.

At the ashram, I am in time for an early lunch—thick rotis made from *mandwa* (millets), two of which are more than enough for me! Endless glasses of milky tea will see me through till supper time.

Towering over Anjani Sain, and blessing all those who live or pass beneath, is the Chanderbadni temple, dedicated to one of the incarnations of the goddess Parvati. As this is not one of the main pilgrim routes, the temple does not get as many visitors as some of the other sacred shrines in the hills. Below the Chanderbadni peak is a rest house, for those who wish to break their journey here.

Anjani Sain lies midway between Tehri and Devprayag—a two-hour bus ride from either place. I came via Tehri, the road climbing steeply above the hot, dusty town that is destined to be submerged by the waters of the Tehri Dam. The dam should have been ready by now, but having been the subject of a great deal of controversy, work on it has progressed in fits and starts.

I am told that this entire region is 'eco-fragile', one of those words bandied around at seminars all over the world. Well, I am not an expert in these matters, (and who is, I wonder) but I should think most of our earth is eco-fragile, having had to put up with hundreds of thousands of years of human civilization.

Do we stop all development in the name of preserving the environment? Or do we move on regardless? 'Proceed with caution' would be the rational person's answer. But are human beings really rational?

Old Tehri was no beauty spot, and New Tehri (growing rapidly above it), is even uglier; from a distance, it looks like a giant cemetery.

When the architecture of suburban Delhi is brought to the hills, what is there to say? You just look the other way.

Fortunately, the defaced mountain is soon left behind, and as it slips out of sight and we ascend into the pine regions, the eye is soothed by the pretty, slate-covered houses of the villages and their little gardens ablaze with marigolds and yellow and bronze chrysanthemums.

Chrysanthemums love this climate. Down in the fields there are patches of crimson *cholai* (amaranth) interspersed with the fresh green of young wheat.

And here are leopards! My companion tells me of one that strolls down the motor road every evening, forcing the local bus to go around him. His presence also accounts for the absence of stray dogs.

Suddenly, in the distance, I see what at first glance appears to be a cloud or a large white sailing ship. On approaching, it turns out to be the freshly white-washed buildings of the Bhuvneshwari Mahila Ashram, clinging to the steep slopes of the mountain.

Here, for two or three days, I find rest and sustenance. The manifold activities of the ashram, (directed mainly towards the welfare of widows and small children) are there for all to see, and I recall the relief work undertaken by its young field workers after the Uttarkashi earthquake last year—they had rushed to the area before the government agencies could swing into action.

However, as a social worker I am somewhat inept. I am just a frazzled old writer who now seeks a refuge from the all-pervasive clutter of tourism that makes ordinary life almost impossible in our hill stations.

I hope the land-grabbers and the real estate 'developers' never get this far. They are welcome to their malls and artificial lakes and concrete parks. Just so long as I am free to escape from it all, to sit here at Anjani Sain contemplating a large white rose in Cyril's garden while the rest of the world watches video.

THE GRAND TRUNK ROAD

There is a fantasy journey that I have always wanted to make, but one that I know I never will: the long, long journey along the Grand Trunk Road from Calcutta to Peshawar.

For the Grand Trunk Road is a river. It may not be as sacred as the Ganga, which it greets at Kanpur and Varanasi, but it is just as permanent. It's a river of life, an unending stream of humanity intent on reaching their destination and getting there most of the time.

A long day's journey into night, that's how I would describe the saga of the truck driver, that knight errant, or rather errant knight, of India's Via Appia. Undervalued, underpaid and often disparaged, he drives all day and sometimes all night, carrying the country's goods and produce for hundreds of miles on the GT Road, across state borders, through lawless tracts, at all seasons and in all weathers. We blame him for hogging the middle of the road, but he is usually overloaded and if he veers too much to the left or right, he is quite likely to topple over, burying himself and his crew under bricks or gas cylinders, sugarcane or TV sets. More than the railway man, the truck driver is modern India's lifeline, and yet his life is held cheap. He drinks, he swears, occasionally he picks up HIV, and frequently he is killed or badly injured. But we cannot do without him.

In the old, old days, when Muhammad Tughlaq, Sultan of

Delhi, streamlined the country's roads, bullock carts and camel caravans were the chief transporters. In 1333, when the Moroccan traveller Ibn Battuta visited India, he was deeply impressed by the Sultan's road network. Sher Shah Suri, who ruled from 1540 till 1545, made further improvements, especially to the GT Road. He built caravanserais and inns for travellers, and planted fine trees along the GT Road and other important highways. Horsemen, carts and palanquin bearers jostled for pride of position, much as our motorists do today. Traffic was slow-moving, and the best way to get ahead was to mount a horse and canter from stage to stage, that is, between 12 and 15 miles a day.

Invading armies had, of course, made use of the Road long before the British gained control of northern India. On this same stretch of the highway, the Persian invader Nadir Shah defeated the Mughal Emperor in 1739. In a battle lasting two hours, over 20,000 of the Emperor's soldiers were killed. The next day, Nadir Shah marched to Delhi, to ransack the city and massacre its inhabitants. The treasure harvest of Delhi was fair game for acquisitive kings and warlords.

When the British consolidated their power in India, they found the Road, stretching as it did from Calcutta to Peshawar, a great line of communication. Kipling's 'regiment a-marchin' down the GT Road' was a common enough sight throughout the nineteenth century. During the 1857 uprising, after the British were ousted from Delhi, their army assembled at Ambala and came marching down the GT Road to lay siege to the city of Delhi. A few years later, a junior officer, recalling the march, wrote:

> The stars were bright in the dark deep sky and the fireflies flashed from bush to bush... Along the road came the heavy roll of the guns, mixed with the jangling of bits

and the clanking of the scabbards of the cavalry. The infantry marched behind with a deep, dull tread. Camels and bullock carts, with innumerable camp servants, toiled away for miles in the rear, while gigantic elephants, pulling the heavy guns, came lumbering down the road.

Some thirty years after the 1857 uprising came the Afghan Wars, and the GT Road became an all-important route for the British army proceeding towards Peshawar and the Khyber Pass. Those were the days of military manoeuvres all over North India, and my grandfather, a foot-soldier in the mould of Kipling's 'soldiers three', found himself 'route marching', that is, foot-slogging all over northern and central India. Wives and children followed the regiment wherever it was sent, and military camps and cantonments sprang up everywhere. Children were often born in the course of these marches and troop movements: my father at Shahjahanpur (not far from the Road), his brothers and sisters at places as far apart as Barrackpore, Campbellpur and Dera Ismail Khan!

The tedium of the march was broken only by the sight of fields of golden corn stretching towards the horizon, with mango groves rising like islands from the flat plain; but for the most part it was monotonous tramping, exemplified in this marching song of Kipling's:

> Oh, there's them Indian temples to admire when you see,
> There's the peacock round the corner
> An' the monkey up the tree.
> With our best foot first
> And the Road a-sliding past,
> An every bloomin' camping-ground
> Exactly like the last.

Kipling immortalized the Road in *Kim* and *Barrack-Room Ballads* (he had a strong empathy with the common soldier); but for him, few outside of India would have heard of the Grand Trunk Road. But Kipling would not recognize the Road today. Cars, buses, tractors, trucks, all thunder down the highway, and even the bullock carts are equipped with heavy tyres. It's a very democratic mix. Nowhere else in the world are you likely to find such a variety of traffic, or so many impediments to vehicular progress—cows, cart-horses, buffaloes, cyclists, stray hens, stray villagers, stray policemen.

'Proceed at your own risk.' You could call this the motto of the Road, a motto vividly illustrated by overturned lorries lying in ditches, buses upended against trees or dangling over culverts, fancy cars crushed into concertina shapes, squashed cats and dogs, mangled drivers and passengers. These are common sights, along with the endless panorama of field, factory, village or township.

For the towns and cities grow bigger by the day. They spread octopus-like over the rural landscape, and the traffic spills out in an endless, honking procession of humankind on wheels. 'OK Tata', proclaims the truck in front of you, and it would be wise to keep your distance. What's your choice of vehicle for making progress on the Road? Motorcycle, taxi, limousine, or buffalo cart? Mine's a steamroller. No one pushes it around.

◆

I have never travelled the entire length of the Road, but I have driven along stretches of it. The most memorable one was with Gurbachan Singh.

As his taxi weaved its way in and out of the Amritsar traffic, and headed for Delhi, Gurbachan Singh took his hand off the horn and gave me a brief triumphant look.

'What do you think of my horn?' he asked.

'Oh, it's a fine horn,' I said, wringing out my ears. 'It couldn't be louder.'

'You can hear it half a mile ahead,' said Gurbachan proudly, as he blasted off at two young men who were sharing a bicycle. They moved out of the way with alacrity.

'It makes a lot of noise in the car, too,' I said, and added hastily, 'not that I object, you know…'

'Doesn't your horn have more than one tone of voice?' asked a fellow traveller with a trace of irritation.

'Two!' claimed Gurbachan. 'Male and female. Just see!' And he produced a high note and then a low note on the horn, both equally ear-shattering. Ahead of us, a tonga ran off the road and on to the cart track.

'This is one terrific horn,' said Gurbachan. I have had it made especially for this taxi. No foreign horns for me. They are not loud enough. Indian horns are best.'

'Indian noise is best,' said the fellow traveller.

In an interval of comparative quiet, I found myself reflecting on the nature of sound—the unpleasantness of some sounds, and the sweetness of others, and why certain sounds (like motor horns) can be sweet to some and hideous to others. The sweetest sound of all, I decided, was silence. There are many kinds of silence—the silence of an empty room, the silence of the mountains, the silence of prayer or the enforced silence of loneliness—but the best kind of silence, I concluded, was the silence that comes after the cessation of noise.

'It was made in the Jama Masjid area,' continued Gurbachan, interrupting my thoughts. 'Seventy-five rupees only. Made by hand, to my own specification. There's only one drawback: it must not get wet!'

As his hand settled down on the horn again, I thought of praying for rain, but the sky being clear and blue, I decided that a prayer would be an unreasonable demand on the Creator.

'Ah, but you don't know what it is to have a horn like this one. Try it, sir. Why don't you try it for yourself?'

'Oh, that's all right,' I assured him. 'You have proved its excellence already.'

'No, you must try it. I insist that you try it!' He was like a big boy, suddenly generous, determined on sharing a new toy with a younger brother.

He grabbed my hand and placed it on the horn, and, as I felt it give a little, a thrill of pleasure rushed up my arm. I pressed hard, and a stream of music flowed in and out of the car. Now I could understand the happiness and the supreme self-confidence of Gurbachan and all drivers like him; for, with a horn like his, one felt the power and glory that belongs to the kings of the road.

For the rest of the journey, Gurbachan drove and I blew the horn.

The fellow passenger, no doubt realizing that he was locked into a taxi with two lunatics, was too terrified to say a word.

RUNNING AWAY

Once, during my schooldays, my friend Daljit and I decided to run away. The main reason for running away was not to get back to the bazaars of Dehra, which we both missed, but to reach my uncle's ship in Jamnagar, Gujarat.

Uncle Jim was one of my father's cousins. He used to write to me off and on throughout the years. His letters came in envelopes that bore colourful stamps of different countries. They came from Valparaiso, San Diego, San Francisco, Buenos Aires, Dar-es-Salaam, Mombasa, Freetown, Singapore, Bombay, Marseilles, London...these were some of the places where Uncle Jim's ship called. He was seldom on the same route, and seemed to move leisurely across the oceans of the earth, calling at ports which had only the most romantic associations for me, for I had already read Stevenson, Captain Marryat, some Conrad and W.W. Jacobs.

In his letters, Uncle Jim often spoke of my joining him at sea—'When you are a little older, Ruskin.'

But I felt I was old enough then. I was sick of school and sick of my guardian. But that was not all. I was in love with the world. I wanted to see the world, every corner of it, the places I had read about in books—the junks and sampans of Hong Kong, the palm-fringed lagoons of the Indies, the streets of London, the beautiful ebony-skinned people of Africa, the bright birds and exotic plants of the Amazon...

When Uncle Jim's last letter had arrived, telling me that his ship would call at Jamnagar towards the end of the month, I felt a deep thrill of anticipation. Here was my chance at last! True, Uncle Jim had said nothing about my joining him, but he was not to know that I was seriously considering it.

It was not simply a question of walking out of school and taking a quick ride down to the docks. Jamnagar, on the west coast, was at least eight hundred miles from my school. I doubt if I would have made the attempt if Daljit had not agreed to come too. It isn't much fun running away on your own. It is even worse if you have a companion who is full of enthusiasm at the beginning and then backs out at the last moment. This leaves one feeling defeated and crushed. Daljit was not that kind of companion. He meant the things he said. About a month earlier, when I had told him of my uncle's ship and my wish to get to it, he had said, without a moment's hesitation: 'I'm coming too!' Daljit lived impulsively. Sometimes, he made mistakes. But he never went halfway and stopped. Someone had to stop him; otherwise he did whatever it was he set out to do.

Running away from school! It is not to be recommended to everyone. Parents and teachers would disapprove. Or would they, deep down in their hearts? Everyone has wanted to run away at some time in his life: if not from a bad school or an unhappy home then from something equally unpleasant. Running away seems to be in the best of traditions. Huck Finn did it. So did Master Copperfield and Oliver Twist. So did Kim. Various enterprising young men have run away to sea. Most great men have run away from school at some stage in their lives; and if they haven't, then perhaps it is something they should have done.

Anyway, Daljit and I ran away from school, and we did it quite successfully too, up to a point. But then, all this happened in India, which, though it forms only two per cent of the world's land mass, has 15 per cent of its population, and so it is an easy place to hide in, or be lost in, or disappear in, and never be seen or heard of again!

Not that we intended to disappear. We were headed for a particular place, and as soon as I took my first step into the unknown, that first step on the slippery pine needles below the school, I knew quite definitely that I wasn't running away from anything, but that I was running *towards* something. Call it a dream, if you like. I was running towards a dream.

A narrow path ran downhill from the school to the road to Dehra, and we followed it until it levelled out, running parallel with the small stream that rumbled down the mountainside. We followed the stream for a mile, walking swiftly and silently, until we met the bridle-path which was little more than a mule-track going steeply down the last hills to the valley.

The going was easy. We knew the road well. And by the time we reached the last foothills, it was beginning to rain, not heavily, but as a light, thin drizzle.

We took shelter in a small dhaba on the outskirts of a village. The dhabawallah was sleeping, and his dog, a mangy pariah with only one ear, sniffed at us in a friendly way instead of chasing us off the premises. We sat down on an old bench and watched the sun rising over the distant mountains.

This is something I have always remembered. Not because it was a more beautiful sunrise than on any other day, but because the special importance of that morning made me look at everything in a new way, hence the details still stand out in my memory.

As the sky grew lighter, the pines and deodars stood out clearly, and the birds came to life. A black-bird started it all with a low, mellow call, and then the thrushes began chattering in the bushes. A barbet shrieked monotonously at the top of a spruce tree, and, as the sky grew lighter still, a flock of bright green parrots flew low over the trees.

The drizzle continued and there was a bright crimson glow in the east. And then, quite suddenly, the sun shot through a gap in the clouds, and the lush green monsoon grass sprang into relief. Both Daljit and I were wonderstruck. Never before had we been up so early. Hundreds of spiderwebs—which were spun in trees and bushes and on the grass, where they would not normally have been noticed—were now clearly visible, spangled with gold and silver raindrops. The strong silk threads of the webs held the light rain and the sun, making each drop of water look like a tiny jewel.

A great wild dahlia, its scarlet flowers drenched and heavy, sprawled over the hillside and an emerald-green grasshopper reclined on a petal, stretching its legs in the sunshine.

The dhabawallah was now up. His dog, emboldened by his master's presence, began to bark at us. The man lit a charcoal fire in a choolah, and put on it a kettle of water to boil.

'Would you like to eat something?' he asked conversationally in Hindi.

'No, just tea for us,' I said.

He placed two brass tumblers on a table.

'The milk hasn't yet been delivered,' he said. 'You're very early.'

'We'll take the tea without milk,' said Daljit. 'But give us lots of sugar.'

'Sugar is costly these days. But because you are schoolboys

and need more, you can help yourselves.'

'Oh, we are not schoolboys,' I said hurriedly.

'Not at all,' added Daljit.

'We are just tourists,' I lied unconvincingly.

'We have to catch the early train at Dehra,' offered Daljit.

'But there's no train before ten o'clock,' said the puzzled dhabawallah.

'It is the ten o'clock train we are catching!' said Daljit smartly. 'Do you think we will be down in time?'

'Oh yes, there's plenty of time...'

The dhabawallah poured out steaming hot tea into the tumblers and placed the sugar bowl in front of us. 'At first I thought you were schoolboys,' he said with a laugh. 'I thought you were running away.'

Daljit almost gave us away by laughing nervously.

'What made you think that?' he asked.

'Oh, I've been here many years,' the dhabawallah replied, gesturing towards the small clearing in which his little wooden stall stood, almost like a trading outpost in a wild country. 'Schoolboys always pass this way when they're running away!'

'Do many run away?' I asked. I felt a little downcast at the thought that Daljit and I were not the first to embark on such an adventure.

'Not many. Just two or three every year. They get as far as the railway station in Dehra and there they're caught!'

'It is silly of them to get caught,' said Daljit disgustedly.

'Are they always caught?' I asked.

'Always! I give them a glass of tea on their way down, and I give them a glass of tea on their way up, when they are returning with their teachers.'

'Well, you won't be seeing *us* again,' said Daljit, ignoring the warning look that I gave him.

'Ah, but you aren't schoolboys!' said the shopkeeper, beaming at us. 'And you aren't running away!'

We paid for our tea and hurried on down the path. The parrots flew over again, screeching loudly, and settled in a lichee tree. The sun was warmer now, and, as the altitude decreased, the temperature and humidity rose and we could almost smell the heat of the plains rising to meet us.

The hills levelled out into the rolling countryside, patterned with fields. Rice had been planted out, and the sugarcane was waist-high.

The path had become quite slushy. Removing our shoes and wrapping them in newspaper, we walked barefoot in the soft mud. All these little out-of-routine acts simply added to our excitement and thrill, making everything quite unforgettable for life.

'It's about three miles into Dehra,' I said. 'We must go round the town. By now, everyone in school will be up and they'll have found out we've gone!'

'We must avoid the Dehra station then,' said Daljit.

'We'll walk to the next station, Raiwala. Then we'll hop onto the first train that comes along.'

'How far must we walk?'

'About ten miles.'

'Ten miles!' Daljit looked dismayed. 'It'll take us all day!'

'Well, we can't stop here nor can we wander about in Dehra, neither can we enter the station. We have to keep on walking.'

'Alright, we'll keep on walking. I suppose the beginning of an adventure is always the most difficult part.'

Soon, the fields were giving way to jungle. But there were still some fields of sugarcane stretching away from the railway lines.

'How much further do we have to walk?' asked Daljit impatiently. 'Is Raiwala in the middle of the jungle?'

'Yes, I think it is. We've covered about four miles I suppose. Six to go! It's funny how some miles seem longer than others. It depends on what one is thinking about, I suppose. If our thoughts are pleasant, the miles are not so long.'

'Then let's keep thinking pleasant thoughts. Isn't there a shortcut anywhere? You've been in these forests before.'

'We'll take the fire-path through the jungle. It'll save us three or four miles. But we'll have to swim or wade across a small river. The rains have only just started, so the water shouldn't be too swift or deep.'

Heavy forests have paths cut through them at various places to prevent forest fires from spreading easily. These paths are not used much by people, since they don't lead anywhere in particular, but they are frequently used by the larger animals.

We had gone about a mile along the path when we heard the sound of rushing water. The path emerged from the forest of sal trees and stopped on the banks of the small river I had mentioned earlier. The main bridge across the river stood on the main road, about three miles downstream.

'It isn't more than waist-deep anywhere,' I said. 'But the water is swift and the stones are slippery.'

We removed our clothes and tied everything into two bundles which we carried on our heads. Daljit was a well-built boy, strong in the arms and thighs. I was slimmer. But I had quick reflexes.

The stones were quite slippery underfoot, and we stumbled, hindering rather than helping each other. We stopped midstream, waist-deep, hesitating about going any further for fear of being swept off our feet.

'I can hardly stand,' said Daljit.

'It shouldn't get worse,' I said hopefully. But the current was strong, and I felt very wobbly in the knees.

Daljit tried to move forward, but slipped and went over backwards into the water, bringing me down too. He began kicking and thrashing about in fear, but eventually, using me as a support, he came up spouting water like a whale.

When we found we were not being swept away, we stopped struggling and cautiously made our way to the opposite bank, but we had been thrust about twenty yards downstream.

We rested on warm sand while a hot sun beat down on us. Daljit sucked at a cut in his hand. But we were soon up and walking again, hungry now, and munching biscuits.

'We haven't far to go,' I said.

'I don't want to think about it,' said Daljit.

We shuffled along the forest path, tired but not discouraged.

Soon we were on the main road again, and there were fields and villages on either side. A cool breeze came in across the open plain, blowing down from the hills. In the fields, there was a gentle swaying movement as the wind stirred the sugarcane. Then, the breeze came down the road, and dust began to swirl and eddy around us. Out of the dust, behind us, came the rumble of cart wheels.

'Ho! Heeyah! Heeyah!' shouted the driver of the cart. The bullocks snorted and came lumbering through the dust. We moved to the side of the road.

'Are you going to Raiwala?' called Daljit. 'Can you take us with you?'

'Climb up!' said the man, and we ran through the dust and clambered on to the back of the moving cart.

The cart lurched forward and rattled and bumped so much

that we had to cling to its sides to avoid falling off. It smelt of grass and mint and cow-dung cakes. The driver had a red cloth tied round his head, and wore a tight vest and a dhoti. He was smoking a beedi and yelling at his bullocks, and he seemed to have forgotten our presence. We were too busy clinging to the sides of the cart to bother about making conversation. Before long we were involved in the traffic of Raiwala—a small but busy market town. We jumped off the bullock cart and walked beside it.

'Should we offer him any money?' I asked.

'No. He will be offended. He is not a taxi driver.'

'Alright, we'll just say thank you.'

We called out our thanks to the cart driver, but he didn't look back. He appeared to be talking to his bullocks.

'I'm hungry,' declared Daljit. 'We haven't had a proper meal since last night.'

'Then let's eat,' I said. 'Come on, Daljit.'

We walked through the small Raiwala bazaar, looking in at the tea and sweet shops until we found the cheapest-looking dhaba. A servant-boy brought us rice and dal and Daljit ordered an ounce of ghee which he poured over the curry. The meal cost us two rupees but we could have as much dal as we wanted, and between us we finished four bowls of it.

'We'll rest at the station,' I said as we emerged from the dhaba. 'We'll buy second-class tickets, and rest in the first-class waiting room. No one will check on us. We look first class, don't we?'

'Not after that walk through the jungle,' replied Daljit.

But we did occupy the best waiting room and Daljit made himself comfortable in an armchair. A train eventually came chugging in, and we were soon on our way to Delhi.

It didn't take us long to find a hotel once we got off at the Old Delhi Railway Station. It was called the Great Oriental Hotel, and was just behind the police station in Chandni Chowk. It didn't pretend to be even a third-class hotel, and for five rupees we were given a small back room which had a window overlooking the godown of an Afghan spice merchant. The powerful smell of asafoetida came up from the courtyard below.

We were tired and hot, so we tossed our belongings down on the floor and took turns at the bathroom tap. Then we stretched out on the only cot in the room and slept through the afternoon, oblivious to the noises from the street, the attentions of the insect population in the hotel mattress, and the creaking of the old fan overhead.

It was late evening when we woke up, and we were hungry again. Daljit opened the door and shouted. Presently, a servant-boy appeared.

'Bring us tea, toast, two big omelettes and a bottle of tomato sauce,' ordered Daljit with a confidence that I wished I had.

The omelettes, when they arrived twenty minutes later, were tiny. Both had obviously been made from one egg. The sauce had been diluted with water, and the toasts were burnt. The salt was damp, and we had to prise open the salt-cellar to get to it. The pepper, however, came out in a generous rush and made up the major portion of the meal. As our hunger had not been satisfied by this poor fare, we ordered eggs again, boiled eggs this time. No matter how tiny, they would have to be whole.

'Let's go out,' said Daljit after we had eaten the eggs. 'It's stuffy in here.'

'I'm still sleepy,' I said.

'Then I'll go out for a little while. I may go to the gurdwara.'

'Alright, but don't get lost.'

Drowsy, I closed my eyes, but the sounds of the city's unceasing traffic came through the window. Ships and distant ports seemed very far away but so did hills and mountain streams.

I fell asleep and woke up only when Daljit returned.

'I've solved our problem!' he said, beaming. 'We won't bother with the train. I met a truck driver, and he has offered to take us as far as Jaipur. That's more than a hundred miles. It will be quite safe to take a train from Jaipur.'

'When can your friend take us?'

'The truck leaves at four o'clock in the morning.'

'There's no rest for the wicked,' I said. 'Still, the less time we lose the better. It's Wednesday, and my uncle's ship might sail on Saturday. What will we have to pay?'

'Nothing. It's a free ride. The driver is a Sikh, and I persuaded him that we are related to each other through the marriage of my brother-in-law to his sister-in-law's niece!'

◆

At four the next morning, we made our way towards the Red Fort, its ramparts dark against the starry sky. The streets which had been teeming with so much life the previous evening were now deserted. The street lamps shed lonely pools of light on the pavements. The occasional car glided silently past, but it belonged to another kind of world altogether.

Near the Fort, we found a couple of dhabas which were still open. They did business with the truck drivers who slept by day and drove by night.

Our driver, a tall, bearded Sikh, loomed over us out of the darkness. He had a companion with him, also a Sikh, who was still in his underwear.

'You can get in at the back,' said the driver in his thick

Punjabi which I could follow sufficiently well. 'We'll be off in a few minutes.'

The truck was parked beneath a peepul tree. We pulled ourselves up into the back of the open truck, only to find our way barred by what seemed at first to be a prehistoric monster.

The monster snorted once, stamped heavily on the boards, and sent us tumbling backwards.

'Bhaiyyaji!' cried Daljit to the driver. 'There's some kind of animal in here!'

'Don't worry, it's only Mumta,' said our friend.

'But what is it doing in here?'

'She is going with us. I am taking her to the market in Jaipur. So get in with her boys, and make yourselves comfortable.'

There was now enough light to enable us to take a closer look at our travelling companion. She was a full-grown buffalo from the Punjab.

'An excellent buffalo,' said Daljit, who appeared to be familiar with the finer points of these animals. 'Notice her blue eyes!'

'I didn't know buffaloes had blue eyes,' I said dryly.

'Only the best buffaloes have them,' said Daljit. 'Blue-eyed buffaloes give more milk than brown-eyed ones.'

Fortunately for us, the Sardarji started the truck and an early morning breeze, blowing across the river, swept away some of the stench so typical of buffaloes.

We were soon out of Delhi and bowling along at a fair speed on the road to Jaipur. The recent rain had waterlogged low-lying areas, and the herons, cranes and snipe were numerous. Fields and trees were alive with strange, beautiful birds: the long-tailed king crow, blue jays and weaver birds, and occasionally the great white-headed kite, which is said to be Garuda, Lord Vishnu's famous steed.

As we travelled further into Rajasthan, the peacocks became more numerous; so did the camels loping along the side of the road in straight, orderly lines. And, as the vegetation grew less and the desert took over, the people themselves grew more colourful, as though to make up for the absence of colour in the landscape. The women wore wide red skirts, and gold and silver ornaments. They were handsome, tall, fair and strong. The men were tall too and the older among them had flowing white beards.

As the day grew older, and the sun rose higher in the sky, the traffic on the road increased; but our truck driver, instead of slowing down, drove faster. Perhaps he was in a hurry to dispose of the buffalo. Soon he was trying to overtake another truck.

The truck in front was moving fast too, and its driver had no intention of giving up the middle of the road. It was piled high with stacks of sugarcane.

'It's going to be a race!' cried Daljit excitedly, standing up against the buffalo, in order to get a better view.

The road was not wide enough to take two large vehicles at once, and as the other truck wouldn't make way, ours had to fall in behind it, almost suffocating us with the exhaust fumes. We were thrown to the floorboards as the truck lurched over the ruts in the rough road, and Mumta, getting nervous, almost trampled us. Then there was a tremendous bump, a grinding of brakes, and we came to a stop.

As the dust cleared, we made out our driver's bearded face gazing anxiously down at us.

'Are you alright?' he asked gruffly.

'I think so,' I said.

'Did you overtake the other truck?' asked Daljit.

'No,' grunted our friend. 'He would not give way. You had better come in front.'

We agreed without any hesitation and his assistant rather grudgingly joined the buffalo.

After a few miles, the driver became friendly and told us that his name was Gurnam Singh.

It was getting dark by the time we reached Jaipur, so we were not able to see much of the city. We spent the night in the truck, sleeping in the back with Gurnam Singh. Mumta had been disposed of on the way. Jaipur nights can be chilly, even in summer, so Gurnam Singh considerately shared his bedding with us. Because he was accustomed to sleeping in the body of the truck, he was soon asleep, snoring loudly and rhythmically. Daljit and I tossed and turned restlessly. He kicked me several times in the night. The floor of the truck was hard, and retained various buffalo smells.

We had hardly fallen asleep (or so it seemed), when Gurnam Singh woke us up, saying that it was almost four o'clock and that he had to start on his return journey, this time with a load of red sandstone.

'What a life!' exclaimed Daljit, sleepily rubbing his eyes with one hand. 'I'd hate to be a truck driver.'

'One has to live somehow,' philosophized Gurnam Singh. 'I like driving. I knew how to drive when I was merely six or seven. The money is not so bad either. Now, when I get back to Delhi, I will have two days off, which I will spend with my wife and children. Goodbye friends, and if you pass through Delhi again, you will find me near the walls of the Red Fort.'

We waved to him as he shot off in his truck, throwing up huge clouds of dust, making a great noise and probably waking the local inhabitants. Dogs barked, and a cock began to crow.

We were on the outskirts of the city, facing a large lake. On the other side was open country, bare hills and desert. We could also make out the ruins of a building—probably a palace or a hunting lodge—among some thorn bushes and babul trees.

'Let's go out there,' suggested Daljit. 'We can bathe in the lake and rest. Then later in the morning we can come into the city and find out about trains.'

We set out along the shores of the lake, and it was a good half-hour before we reached the opposite bank.

There was no one in the fields, but a camel was going round and round a well, drawing up water in small trays. Smoke rose from houses in a nearby village, and the notes of a flute floated over to us on the still morning air.

It took us about twenty minutes to reach the ruin, which seemed like an old hunting lodge put up by some Rajput prince when game must have been plentiful.

The gate of the lodge was blocked with rubble, but part of the wall had crumbled apart and we climbed through the gap and found ourselves in a stone-paved courtyard in the centre of which stood a dry, disused stone fountain. A small peepul tree was growing from the crack in the floor of the fountain. Finding nothing to do there, we made our way to the railway tracks again.

Daljit and I snuck on to a goods train. It was a hard night's journey. The train was agonizingly slow and stopped at many places. At one small station, a number of sacks filled with what must have been cattle-fodder were tossed into the wagon, almost burying us in our fitful sleep. But we found they were comfortable to rest on and lay stretched out on top of them until the first light of morning.

As the sky cleared, we knew we were not far from our journey's end. The landscape had undergone a complete change. We had left the desert for the coastal plain.

The tall waving palms parted, and then I spotted the sea.

It was the sea as I had always dreamt of it ever since my days in Kathiawar with my father. It was vast, lonely and blue, blue as the sky was blue, and the first ship I saw was a sailing-ship, an Arab dhow, listing slightly in the mild breeze that blew onto the shore.

The train stopped at a small bridge spanning a stream which wound its way across the plain down to the sea. We got down there and trudged the rest of the way to our destination.

Two hours later, we were at Jamnagar.

We stopped near a small tea shop and watched other people eating laddoos and bhelpuri. We couldn't even afford a coconut.

'Where is the harbour?' I asked the shopkeeper.

'Two miles from here,' he replied.

'Are there any ships in the port?' I asked, relieved yet anxious.

'What do you want with a ship?'

'What does anyone want with a ship?'

'Well there's only one and it sails today, so you had better hurry if you want to go away on it.'

'Let's go,' said Daljit.

'Wait!' said a young man who was lounging against the counter. 'It will take you almost an hour to get there if you walk. I will take you in my cart.' He pointed to a shabby pony cart close by. The pony did not look as though it wanted to go anywhere.

'My pony is fast!' said the young man, following our glances. 'Never go by appearances. She may look tired but she runs like a champion! Get in friends, I will charge you only one rupee.'

'We don't have any money,' I said. 'We'll walk.'

'Fifty paisa, then,' he said. 'Fifty paisa and a glass of tea. Jump in my friends!'

'All right,' agreed Daljit. 'There's no time to lose. Fifty paisa and buy your own tea.'

We climbed into the cart, and the youth jumped up in front and cracked his whip. The pony lurched forward, the wheels rattled and shook, and we set off down the bazaar road at a tremendous trot.

'I didn't know you had fifty paisa left,' I said.

'I don't,' Daljit replied. 'But we'll worry about that later. Your uncle can pay!'

As soon as we were out of the town and on the open road to the sea, the pony went faster. She couldn't help doing so, as the road was downhill. The wind blew my hair across my eyes, and the salty tang of the sea was in the air.

Daljit shook me in his excitement.

'We will soon be at the harbour,' he yelled joyfully. 'And then away at last!'

The driver called out endearments to his pony, and, exhilarated by the sea breeze and the comparative speed of his carriage, he burst into song. As we turned a bend in the road, the sea-front came into view. There were several small dhows close to the shore, and fishing-boats were beached on the sand. The fishermen were drying their nets while their children ran naked in the surf. A steamer stood out on the sea and though I could not make out its name from that distance, I was sure it was the *Iris*.

The cart stopped at the beginning of the pier, and we tumbled out and began running along the pier. But even as we ran, it became clear to me that the ship was moving away from us, moving out to the sea. Its propeller sent small waves rippling back to the pier.

'Captain!' I shouted. 'Uncle Jim! Wait for us!'

A lascar standing in the stern waved to us; but that was all.

I stood at the end of the pier, waving my hands and shouting into the wind.

'Captain! Uncle Jim! Wait for us!'

Nobody answered. The seagulls, wheeling in the wake of the steamer, seemed to take up the cry—'Captain, Captain...'

The ship drew further away, gaining speed. And still I called to it in a hoarse, pleading voice. Yokohama, San Diego, Valparaiso, London, all slipped away forever...

WALKING THE STREETS OF DELHI

I made my home in Mussoorie in 1963, but of course I was to revisit Delhi many times, even spending a couple of winters there.

On one of these visits, in 1971, I reached my friend Kamal's house in Rajouri Garden, and mentioned that I had walked from Connaught Place, a distance of some eight miles. His family greeted me with a pained and bewildered silence.

Finally my friend's mother, a practical Punjabi lady, asked: 'How did you lose your money?' She kept hers knotted in the end of her sari, and firmly believed that people who kept their money in easily snatched handbags and wallets were asking for trouble.

'I haven't lost anything,' I said.

'Aren't the buses running?'

'Oh, the buses are running. One nearly ran over me.'

'Then why did you walk?'

'I thought I'd see more that way.'

The rest of the story is told in my journal.

The consensus of opinion in my friend's house is that I am a little mad. They have never heard of anyone in Delhi walking by choice. They prefer to wait long periods for overcrowded buses and hang on by their eyebrows, even if the distance to be covered is only a furlong. As in big cities the world over, the people of Delhi are rapidly losing the use of their legs.

I suppose Delhi is one of the least attractive cities in which to walk about. Crossing roads can be hazardous. Single and double-decker buses (many emitting smokescreens of diesel fumes), wildly driven taxis, unpredictable scooter-rickshaws, slow-moving cars and tongas, and thousands of wavering, wayward cyclists, make for chaos on the streets. On the main roads, the traffic is fast and furious, and cyclists are frequently knocked over and killed. But Delhi has an acute transport problem, and the cycle is the poor man's only guarantee of getting to work in time. He cannot afford a scooter, and he cannot wait for a bus. And yet, in this city bursting with the Punjabi nouveau riche, there are thousands who do have their own scooters and cars, and the number and variety of vehicles on the road increase at an alarming rate.

Setting out on another long walk, I realized that the pavement is meant for almost every purpose except walking. I was on the Najafgarh Road, heading in the general direction of central Delhi. It is a straight road, but this is no straight walk. To find a thirty-yard stretch of unoccupied pavement is most unlikely. In a territory where every square foot of land has a high price, why should so much good pavement go to waste?

The first two wayside stalls belong to sellers of lottery tickets. Theirs is a thriving business. All over Delhi, at almost every street corner, there is someone selling lottery tickets. The prizes are attractive enough. The owner of the winning ticket collects ₹250,000—sometimes more—and there are a number of other prizes. And the income accruing to the state is also tremendous—so much so that almost every state in the country, including Delhi, has climbed on the lottery bandwagon. After all, it is easier than collecting taxes. No one, not even the street sweeper, grudges giving a rupee to the government if there is a chance in a million of his winning a fortune.

While the poor man is quite willing to part with his rupee, it is the rich man, the thriving businessman, who often goes in for lottery tickets in a big way, sometimes buying up forty or fifty tickets at a time. He believes that while it is great to be rich, there is nothing like getting richer.

How times have changed. Ten years ago, if I asked a Sikh boy what he would like to be on growing up, he would unhesitatingly have said, 'I'll join the Army'—or the Navy or the Air Force. He would have been proud of his martial traditions. Yesterday, while talking to an intelligent twelve-year-old Sikh, I asked the same question and received this reply: 'I'll open a cinema or deal in spare parts.'

No spirit of adventure, no vision of faraway places—unless it be of a cloth shop in Bangkok! The boy confessed that what he really wanted in life was a television set bigger and better than his neighbour's.

But Delhi is not entirely Punjabi. Here, on the Najafgarh Road, I find a community of Lohiawalas, a gypsy tribe of blacksmiths who have wandered into Delhi, camped on the pavement, and gone about their ancient and traditional way of living, supremely indifferent to the fast pace, the noise of traffic, the neon signs and Western clothes that surround them on all sides. Their bullock-carts (in which they travel and sleep and live and die and have their babies) stand just off the pavement; these are lined with old iron, stamped with decorative patterns and studded with coloured stones.

A charcoal fire has been made in a hole in the ground, and this is kept alive by a bellows worked by a wheel that an attractive woman wearing a black blouse and black skirt was turning.

This sombre attire is set off by heavy silver anklets and a pair of very lively eyes. Another pair of bellows has been fashioned out of goat's skin. A man is beating out a strip of red-hot tin on his anvil. A boy is filling a bent bicycle-pump with sand (to keep it firm) before straightening it out with his hammer. The entire family—including bearded old men, wizened old women ready to take off on broomsticks, and naked grandchildren—is at work. Handsome people these; and although they live in dirt and squalor, they seem quiet and dignified.

A little farther along the road are some people making what appear to be straw mats. These turn out to be roofs for the small shacks belonging to the Rajasthani labourers who live on the other side of an open drain. The walls of these shacks are about four feet high, the rooms about six feet square. There is no sanitation. People use the drain. They bathe at a public tap. During the rains, water moves sluggishly along this drain, but now it is dry except for pools of stagnant, slimy water, a grey liquid tinged with green. It must hold treasures for anyone searching for biological specimens. (And indeed, the enterprising Delhiwala has not ignored this possibility, for farther along, on Link Road, frogs are on sale to biology students.)

At this side of the road lies a dead pony, knocked down at night by a speeding truck. A portion has been eaten away by dogs and jackals. It is now being pecked at by crows; when these birds tire of the stinking carcass, they move on to a nearby fruit stall. No one seems to notice this, least of all the fruit vendors. Well-dressed people pass by without a glance at the dead horse or the open drain. Is it apathy, or is it that Delhi people—city people—are unobservant by nature? Does city life dull the perceptions? Are the giant cinema hoardings so overpowering, so dazzling, that everything else pales into insignificance beside them?

Some of the shack-dwellers have tried to make their homes attractive. They have whitewashed their walls, adorned them with crude but colourful drawings of birds and animals. But what a contrast there is between these humble homes and the elegant villas and bungalows of Kirti Nagar, Patel Nagar and Pusa Road, three prosperous areas of Delhi which lie on my route. A tenant has to pay anything from ₹300–500 a month for a small flat in one of these fine houses.

I went flat hunting once, but I was turned away by the house owners—not because of race, colour or religion, but because I was a bachelor. In India, staying single is something of a crime against society. Bachelors have a rough time; they seldom get invited into homes where there are girls of marriageable age.

'Are Delhi bachelors such monsters?' I asked a house agent in Rajinder Nagar.

'Most of them are very well-behaved,' he said. 'But you see, parents no longer have much confidence in their daughters. A girl sees too many films, and then she wants to have a tragic affair with the first good-looking male who comes along.'

It has taken me two hours of foot-slogging to reach Connaught Place, which is still the premier shopping centre of New Delhi, I remember it well from my childhood, in the war years, when my father was stationed at Air Headquarters in New Delhi. The capital was a small, sparsely populated town in those days. We lived in temporary RAF hutments on Wellesley Road. A multi-storeyed hotel now occupies the site. The jungle where I hunted rabbits has long since been cleared to make way for the expensive residential area of Sunder Nagar. But the central vista, leading from India Gate up to Lutyens's complex of Parliament

House and the President's Estate, is still a lovely stretch of green grass, still water and shady jamun trees.

Connaught Place has not changed much. The milk bar I frequented as a boy is still there, although they do not sell milk any more; now it is espresso coffee and hamburgers. The Regal cinema has switched over to Hindi films. In its cellar is a discotheque. Shopfronts are more flashy, but service-lanes have not altered. And of course the faces and clothes are different. The British uniforms of the war years have given way to the uniforms of the hippies, who slouch about in beads and togas, unaccepted and even scorned by the local citizens. Indians are not impressed by people who do not dress well. Their concept of the true Englishman is of the sahib who dresses for dinner even when there is no dinner; they *like* that kind of Englishman. No one is as clothes-conscious as a Punjabi. He likes his shoes polished, his shirt pressed, his suit spotless—a difficult business in Delhi, where the dust, even in winter, is as thick as in the time of Emperor Shah Jahan who, proud of his new capital, asked the Persian Ambassador how it compared with his Isphahan, and received the double-edged reply: 'By God! Isphahan cannot be compared with the dust of your Delhi!'

But Shah Jahan's Delhi, the old walled city near the Yamuna, is not on my route today. I am tired and hungry, and I lunch at a dhaba, a cheap eating-house, one of many lining the outer pavements round Connaught Place. If one does not mind the filthy surroundings, there is good meat to be had in these little restaurants, most of them run by Punjabis who learned their cooking in Lahore. Certainly the food here is better and cheaper than the watered-down dishes served in some of the smart restaurants in the inner circle. The dish-washers and servers are barefooted hill boys, working in the city because their small fields in the hills do not provide a sufficient living for their families. They work quite cheerfully (for they are cheerful by nature), in spite of hard words, cuffs and meagre wages.

Outside, on the road, a small crowd has gathered round a turbaned Pathan. For a moment I fear violence for this exotic stranger; then I realize that the crowd is merely curious, even in good humour. The Pathan is extolling the virtues of an aphrodisiac mixture which he is trying to sell. 'Be happy!' he cries. 'And make your bulbul happy!'

In spite of the family planning hoarding directly behind him, he appears to be doing good business. It is, after all, the wedding season.

I am forcibly reminded of this on my way home in the evening. The roads in and out of every residential area are blocked by shamianas put up for wedding receptions. This is illegal, but the fine is a small one, and when a father is spending thousands on his daughter's wedding, he dosen't mind paying a fine of ₹40. He accepts the summons with good humour, and carries on with the reception. This is the month most propitious for marriages. After 15 January, four months must pass before a Hindu will marry off his daughter. Astrology plays as great a part in the lives of the people here today as it did three hundred years ago when the traveller Francois Bernier observed that no one in Delhi, Hindu or Muslim, undertook any project without first consulting his astrologer. Today, matchmakers must still study the stars in their courses before pairing a boy with a girl.

Most fathers love to give their daughters a good send-off, and Delhi marriages are splendid, glittering affairs. The bridegroom traditionally arrives on a white horse, but Delhiwalas, who like being up-to-date, often use cars, jeeps or even tractors (because of the high perch they provide).

I find myself involved in a procession on Pusa Road. It is impossible to get past the throng of people, so I must remain with them for some distance. If I choose to attend the reception, no one will turn me away. The bride's people will be under the impression that I am one of the bridegroom's guests, and the bridegroom's group will feel sure that I belong to the bride's party. As most of the guests are seeing each other for the first time, it is possible for any well-dressed person to join the festivities. This frequently happens.

There has, of course, to be a band, and bands are chosen mainly on the strength of the volume of noise they are able to produce and sustain. A trumpet, sounding a foot away from my ear, sends me reeling to the rear of the procession. Drums, bugles, clarinets and saxophones burst into a great profanity of sound. It is not Indian music they play, but a combination of military marches and popular Hindi film tunes. There is nothing like it anywhere else on earth.

The bandsmen wear red coats and white spats, but shoes are optional. On their heads, they wear what appear to be Salvation Army caps. They will play on their instruments (often independently of each other) for as long as they are paid to play, and must deliver a final burst at daybreak when the bride leaves her father's house.

It is a colourful procession, headed by small urchin boys carrying gas lamps. After them comes the band; then the bridegroom's beautifully clothed friends and relatives; and finally the bridegroom, enthroned on top of a gaily caparisoned jeep.

I take a side road and leave the procession, but find my way blocked by another marriage party. This time a heavily-built Sikh, slightly tipsy, embraces me as a long-lost brother. He seems to know me. Quite possibly I knew him when he was a smooth-cheeked lad of fifteen; but now, disguised by a magnificent beard, he reminds me of no one I have ever known. But he wants me to join his party, and so, to humour him, I accompany him for about a hundred yards, when he suddenly forgets me and rushes off to some other old acquaintance.

I have to reconnoitre another three processions, and four more shamianas, before I reach Rajouri Garden. I keep going by eating boiled eggs. These are sold on the roadside, and the egg-seller will even peel the egg for you, and serve it sliced, with pepper and salt, on a piece of newspaper. Unfortunately all the egg-sellers disappear when summer comes, because people believe that eggs are 'heating' and should only be eaten during the winter months. I suppose the same reasoning applies to the Pathan's tonic mixture. I am almost home. It does not look as though anyone in Delhi sleeps at night, but I am ready for bed, and all the brass bands in the city (and there must be over a hundred of them) will not keep me from sleeping.

But there is something I must do first.

The seller of lottery tickets has been staring hopefully at me, and I hate to disappoint him last thing at night. So I produce a rupee and buy a ticket; and, in doing so, I feel that I have finally identified myself with the good people of Delhi.

STREET OF THE RED WELL

The sun beats down on the sweltering city of Old Delhi. Not a breath of air stirs in the narrow, winding streets. This old walled city, now over three hundred years old, has no open spaces, no sidewalks, no shady avenues. During the reign of Emperor Shah Jahan, a canal ran down the centre of the main thoroughfare, Chandni Chowk (street of the silversmiths), but the canal has long since been covered over, and the Yamuna river, from which water has been channelled, lies beyond the emperor's fort, the Red Fort of Delhi, where the prime minister speaks to the multitude every year on Independence Day.

It is not water that I seek most, but shelter from the heat and glare of the overhead sun. I have chosen what is quite possibly the hottest day in May, the temperature over 105 degrees Fahrenheit, to go walking in search of—what? A story, perhaps, and adventure. Or that is what I set out to do. The heat of the day has willed otherwise. I may be ready for an adventure, but no one else is interested. I am the only one walking the streets from choice.

Shopkeepers nod drowsily beneath whirring ceiling fans. The pavement barber has taken his customer into the shelter of an awning. A fortune-teller has decided that there is nothing to predict and has fallen asleep under the same awning. A vegetable seller sprinkles water on his vegetables in a dispirited fashion.

Those cauliflowers were fresh an hour ago: they look old already. Even the flies are drowsy. Instead of buzzing feverishly from place to place, they stagger about on tired legs.

It is the pigeons who have found all the coolest places. These birds have made the old city their own. New Delhi is for the crows who like to have a tree to sleep in, even if they take their meals from out of kitchens and verandahs. But the pigeons prefer buildings, and the older the buildings the better. They are familiar with every cool alcove or shady recess in the crumbling walls of neglected mosques and mansions.

A fat, supercilious pigeon watches me from the window ledge above a jeweller's shop. The pigeon's forebears settled here long before the British thought of taking Delhi. Conquerors have come and gone, Nadir Shah the Persian, Madhav Rao the Maratha, Gulam Kadir the Rohilla and generations of goldsmiths and silversmiths. Hindus and Muslims have made and lost fortunes in the city, but nothing has disturbed the tranquil life of these pigeons. Their gentle cooing can always be heard when there is a lull in the jagged symphony of traffic noise. How do they manage to sound so cool?

But here's welcome relief for humans; a shady corner in Lal Kuan bazaar (street of the Red Well), where an old man provides drinking water to thirsty wayfarers such as myself. His water is stored in a surahi, an earthenware jug which keeps the water sweet and cool. I bend down, cup my hands and receive the sparkling liquid as my benefactor tilts the surahi towards me.

Lal Kuan. The Red Well. Of course it is no longer here, but the street still bears its name. And I like to think that here, in the middle of the street, where a bullock has gone to sleep, forcing the cyclists to make a detour, there was once a well, made of dark red brick, where the water bubbled forth all day. Imprisoned beneath the soil, held down by the crowded commercial houses of this old quarter, the water must still be there; it gives nourishment to an old peepul tree that grows beside a temple. It is the only tree on the street. It juts out from the temple wall growing straight and tall, dwarfing the two-storeyed houses. One of its roots, breaking throughout the ground, has curled up to provide a smooth, well-worn seat. And it is cool here, beneath the peepul.

On the other side of the road, a tall iron doorway is set in a high wall. Doors like this were only built in the previous century, when a wealthy merchant's house had to be a miniature fortress as well as a residence. I cannot see over the wall and I would like to know what lies behind the door. Perhaps a side street, perhaps a market, perhaps a garden, perhaps...

The door opens, not easily, because it had been left closed for a long time, but slowly and with much complaint. And beyond the door, there is only an empty courtyard, covered with rubble, the ruins of the old house. I am about to turn away when I hear a deep tremendous murmur.

It is the cooing of many pigeons. But where are they?

I advance further into the ruin, and there, opening out in front of me, ready to receive me as the rabbit hole was ready to receive Alice, is an old, disused well. I peer down into its murky depths. It is dark, very dark down there; but that is where the pigeons live, in the walls of this lost, long-forgotten well shut away from the rest of the city. I cannot see any water, so I drop a pebble over the side. It strikes the wall, and then, with a soft plop, touches water. At that instant, there is a rush of air and a tremendous beating of wings, and a flock of pigeons—thirty or forty of them—fly out of the well, streak upwards, circle the building, and then falling into formation, wheel overhead, the sun gleaming white on their underwings.

I have discovered their secret. Now I know why they look so cool, so refreshed, while we who walk the streets of Old Delhi do so with parched mouths and drooping limbs. The pigeons are the only ones who still know about the Red Well.

THE ROAD TO BADRINATH

If you have travelled up the Mandakini valley, and then crossed over into the valley of the Alaknanda, you are immediately struck by the contrast. The Mandakini is gentler, richer in vegetation, almost pastoral in places; the Alaknanda is awesome, precipitous, threatening—and seemingly inhospitable to those who must live and earn a livelihood, in its confines.

Even as we left Chamoli and began the steady, winding climb to Badrinath, the nature of the terrain underwent a dramatic change. No longer did green fields slope gently down to the riverbed. Here, they clung precariously to rocky slopes and ledges that grew steeper and narrower, while the river below, impatient to reach its confluence with the Bhagirathi at Deoprayag, thundered along the narrow gorge.

Badrinath is one of the four dhams, or four most holy places in India. (The other three are Rameshwaram, Dwarka and Jagannath Puri.) For the pilgrim travelling to this holiest of holies, the journey is exciting, possibly even uplifting; but for those who live permanently on these crags and ridges, life is harsh, a struggle from one day to the next. No wonder so many young men from Garhwal find their way into the army. Little grows on these rocky promontories; and whatever does, is at the mercy of the weather. For most of the year, the fields lie fallow. Rivers, unfortunately, run downhill and not uphill.

The harshness of this life, typical of much of Garhwal, was brought home to me at Pipalkoti, where we stopped for the night. Pilgrims stop here by the coachload, for the Garhwal Mandal Vikas Nigam's rest house is fairly capacious, with small hotels and dharamshalas abound. Just off the busy road is a tiny hospital, and here, late in the evening, we came across a woman keeping vigil over the dead body of her husband. The body had been laid out on a bench in the courtyard. A few feet away, the road was crowded with pilgrims in festival mood; no one glanced over the low wall to notice this tragic scene.

The woman came from a village near Helong. Earlier that day, finding her consumptive husband in a critical condition, she had decided to bring him to the nearest town for treatment. As he was frail and emaciated, she was able to carry him on her back for several miles, until she reached the motor road. Then, at some expense, she engaged a passing taxi and brought him to Pipalkoti. But he was already dead when she reached the small hospital. There was no morgue; so she sat beside the body in the courtyard, waiting for dawn and the arrival of others from the village. A few men arrived next morning and we saw them wending their way down to the cremation ground. We did not see the woman again. Her children were hungry and she had to hurry home to look after them.

Pipalkoti is hot (and peepul trees are conspicuous by their absence), but Joshimath, the winter resort of the Badrinath temple establishment, is about 6,000 feet above sea level and has an equable climate. It is now a fairly large town, and although the surrounding hills are rather bare, it does have one great tree that has survived the ravages of time. This is an ancient mulberry, known as the Kalpa Vriksha (Immortal Wishing Tree), beneath which the great Sankaracharya meditated, a few centuries ago. It is reputedly over 2,000 years old, and is certainly larger than my modest four-roomed flat in Mussoorie. Sixty pilgrims holding hands might just about encircle its trunk.

I have seen some big trees, but this is certainly the oldest and broadest of them. I am glad the Sankaracharya meditated beneath it and thus ensured its preservation. Otherwise, it might well have gone the way of other great trees and forests that once flourished in this area.

A small boy reminds me that it is a wishing tree, so I make my wish. I wish that other trees might prosper like this one.

'Have you made a wish?' I ask the boy.

'I wish that you will give me one rupee,' he says. His wish comes true with immediate effect. Mine lies in the uncertain future. But he has given me a lesson in wishing.

Joshimath has to be a fairly large place because most of Badrinath arrives here in November, when the shrine is snowbound for six months. Army and PWD structures also dot the landscape. This is no carefree hill resort, but it has all the amenities for making a short stay quite pleasant and interesting. Perched on the steep mountainside above the junction of the Alaknanda and Dhauli rivers, it is now vastly different from what it was when Frank Smythe visited it fifty years ago and described it as 'an ugly little place...straggling unbeautifully over the hillside. Primitive little shops line the main street, which is roughly paved in places and in others has been deeply channelled by the monsoon rains. The pilgrims spend the night in single-storeyed rest houses, not unlike the hovels provided for the Kentish hop-pickers of former days, some of which are situated in narrow passages running off the main street and are filthy and evil-smelling'.

Those were Joshimath's former days. It is a different place

today, with small hotels, modern shops, a cinema hall; and its growth and comparative modernity date from the early sixties, when the old pilgrim footpath gave way to the motor road which takes the traveller all the way to Badrinath. No longer does the weary, footsore pilgrim sink gratefully down in the shade of the Kalpa Vriksha. He alights from his bus or luxury coach and drinks a cola or a Thums-up at one of the many small restaurants on the roadside.

Contrast this comfortable journey with the pilgrimage fifty years ago. Frank Smythe had said: 'So they venture on their pilgrimage... Some borne magnificently by coolies, some toiling along in rags, some almost crawling, preyed on by disease and distorted by dreadful deformities... Europeans who have read and travelled cannot conceive what goes on in the minds of these simple folk, many of them from the agricultural parts of India, wonderment and fear must be the prime ingredients. So the pilgrimage becomes an adventure. Unknown dangers threaten the broad, well-made path, at any moment the gods, who hold the rocks in leash, may unloose their wrath upon the hapless passer-by. To the European it is a walk to Badrinath, to the Hindu pilgrim it is far, far more.'

Above Vishnuprayag, Smythe left the Alaknanda and entered the Bhyundar valley, a botanist's paradise, which he called the Valley of Flowers. He fell in love with the lush meadows of this high valley, and made it known to the world. It continues to attract the botanist and trekker. Primulas of subtle shades, wild geraniums, saxifrages clinging to the rocks, yellow and red potentillas, snow-white anemones, delphiniums, violets, wild roses, all these and many more flourish there, capturing the mind and heart of the flower lover.

'Impossible to take a step without crushing a flower.' This

may not be true any more, for many footsteps have trodden Bhyundar in recent years. There are other areas in Garhwal where the hills are rich in flora—the Har-ki-doon, Harsil, Tungnath, and the Khirai valley where the balsam grows to a height of eight feet—but Bhyundar has both a variety and a concentration of wild flowers, especially towards the end of the monsoon. It would be no exaggeration to call it one of the most beautiful valleys in the world. Bhyundar is a digression for lovers of mountain scenery; but the pilgrim keeps his eyes fixed on the ultimate goal—Badrinath, where the gods dwelt and where salvation is to be found.

There are still a few who do it the hard way—mostly those who have taken sanyas and renounced the world. Here is one hardy soul doing penance. He stretches himself out on the ground, draws himself up to a standing position, then flattens himself out again. In this manner, he will proceed from Badrinath to Rishikesh, oblivious of the sun and rain, the dust from passing buses, the sharp gravel of the footpath.

Others are not so hardy. One saffron-robed scholar, speaking fair English, asks us for a lift to Badrinath, and we find a space for him. He rewards us with a long and involved commentary on the Vedas, which lasts through the remainder of the journey. His special field of study, he informs us, is the part played by aeronautics in Vedic literature.

'And what,' I ask him, 'is the connection between the two?'

He looks at me pityingly.

'It is what I am trying to find out,' he replies.

The road drops to Pandukeshwar and rises again, and all the time I am scanning the horizon for the forests of the Badrinath region I had read about many years ago in James B. Fraser's *The Himalaya Mountains*! Walnuts growing up to 9,000 feet, deodars and 'bilka' up to 9,500 feet, and 'amesh' and 'kiusu' fir up a similar height—but, apart from strands of long-leaved excelsa pine, I do not see much, certainly no deodars. What has happened to them, I wonder. An endless variety of trees delighted us all the way from Dugalbeta to Mandal, a well-protected area, but here on the high ridges above the Alaknanda, little seems to grow; or, if ever they did, they have long since been bespoiled or swept away.

Finally we reach the wind-swept, barren valley which harbours Badrinath—a growing township, thriving, lively, but somewhat dwarfed by the snow-capped peaks that tower above it. As at Joshimath, there is no dearth of hostelries and dharamshalas. Even so, every hotel or rest house is filled to overflowing capacity. It is the height of the pilgrim season, and pilgrims, tourists and mendicants of every description throng the riverfront.

Just as Kedar is the most sacred of the Shiva temples in the Himalayas, Badrinath is the supreme place of worship for the Vaishnav sects.

According to legend, when Sankaracharya in his digvijaya travels visited the Mana valley, he arrived at the Narada–Kund and found fifty different images lying in its waters. These he rescued, and when he had done so, a voice from heaven said, 'These are the images for the Kaliyug, establish them here.' Sankaracharya accordingly placed them beneath a mighty tree which grew there and whose shade extended from Badrinath to Nandprayag, a distance of over eighty miles. Close to it was the hermitage of Nar-Narayana (or Arjuna and Krishna), and over time, temples were built in honour of these and other manifestations of Vishnu. It was here that Vishnu appeared to his followers in person as the four-armed, crested and adorned with pearls and garlands. The faithful, it is said, can still see him on the peak of Nilkantha, on the great Kumbha day. It is, in fact, the Nilkantha peak that dominates this crater-like valley where a few hardy thistles and nettles manage to survive. Like cacti in the desert, the pricklier forms of life seem best equipped to live in a hostile environment.

Nilkantha means blue-necked, an allusion to Shiva's swallowing of a poison meant to destroy the world. The poison remained in his throat, which was rendered blue thereafter. It is a majestic and awe-inspiring peak, soaring to a height of 21,640 feet. As its summit is only five miles from Badrinath, it is justly held in reverence. From its ice-clad pinnacle, three great ridges sweep down, of which the southern one terminates in the Alaknanda valley.

On the evening of our arrival, we could not see the peak, as it was hidden in clouds. Badrinath itself was shrouded in mist. But we made our way to the temple, a gaily decorated building about fifty feet high, with a gilded roof. The image of Vishnu, carved in black stone, stands in the centre of the sanctum, opposite the door, in a dhyana posture. An endless stream of people passes through the temple to pay homage and emerge better for their proximity to the divine.

From the temple, flights of steps lead down to the rushing river and to the hot springs which emerge just above it. Another road leads through a long but tidy bazaar where pilgrims may buy mementos of their visit—from sacred amulets to pictures of the gods in vibrant technicolour. Here at last, I am free to indulge my passion for cheap rings, with none to laugh at my foible. There are all kinds, from rings designed like a coiled serpent (my favourite) to twisted bands of copper and iron and others containing the pictures of gods, gurus and godmen.

They do not cost more that two or three rupees each, and so I am able to fill my pockets. I never wear these rings. I simply hoard them away. My friends are convinced that in a previous existence, I was a jackdaw, seizing upon and hiding away any kind of bright and shiny object: So be it...

Even those who have renounced the world appear to be cheerful—like the young woman from Gujarat who had taken sanyas and who met me on the steps below the temple. She gave me a dazzling smile and passed me an exercise book. She had taken a vow of silence; but being, I think, of an extrovert nature, she seemed eager to remain in close communication with the rest of humanity, and did so by means of written questions and answers. Hence, the exercise book

Although at Badrinath, I missed the sound of birds and the presence of trees, it was good to be part of the happy throng at its colourful little temple, and to see the sacred river close to the source. And early next morning I was rewarded with the liveliest experience of all.

Opening the window of my room, and glancing out, I saw the rising sun touch the snow-clad summit of Nilkantha. At first, the snows were pink; then they turned to orange and gold. All sleep vanished as I gazed up in wonder at that magnificent pinnacle in the sky. And had Lord Vishnu appeared just then on the summit, I would not have been in the least surprised.

A NIGHT WALK HOME

No night is so dark as it seems.

Here in Landour, on the first range of the Himalayas, I have grown accustomed to the night's brightness—moonlight, starlight, lamplight, firelight! Even fireflies light up the darkness.

Over the years, the night has become my friend. On the one hand, it gives me privacy; on the other, it provides me with limitless freedom.

Not many people relish the dark. There are some who will even sleep with their lights burning all night. They feel safer that way. Safer from the phantoms conjured up by their imaginations. A primeval instinct, perhaps, going back to the time when primitive man hunted by day and was in turn hunted by night.

And yet, I have always felt safer by night, provided I do not deliberately wander about on clifftops or roads where danger is known to lurk. It's true that burglars and lawbreakers often work by night, their principal object being to get into other people's houses and make off with the silver or the family jewels. They are not into communing with the stars. Nor are late-night revellers, who are usually to be found in brightly lit places and are thus easily avoided. The odd drunk stumbling home is quite harmless and probably in need of guidance.

I feel safer by night, yes, but then I do have the advantage of living in the mountains, in a region where crime and random violence are comparatively rare. I know that if I were living in a big city in some other part of the world, I would think twice about walking home at midnight, no matter how pleasing the night sky would be.

Walking home at midnight in Landour can be quite eventful, but in a different sort of way. One is conscious all the time of the silent life in the surrounding trees and bushes. I have smelt a leopard without seeing it. I have seen jackals on the prowl. I have watched foxes dance in the moonlight. I have seen flying squirrels flit from one treetop to another. I have observed pine martens on their nocturnal journeys and listened to the calls of nightjars and owls and other birds who live by night. Not all on the same night, of course. That would be a case of too many riches all at once. Some night walks can be uneventful. But usually there is something to see or hear or sense. Like those foxes dancing in the moonlight. One night, when I got home, I sat down and wrote these lines:

> As I walked home last night,
> I saw a lone fox dancing
> In the bright moonlight.
> I stood and watched; then
> Took the low road, knowing
> The night was his by right.
> Sometimes, when words ring true,
> I'm like a lone fox dancing
> In the morning dew.

Who else, apart from foxes, flying squirrels and night-loving writers are at home in the dark? Well, there are the nightjars, not much to look at, although their large, lustrous eyes gleam uncannily in the light of a lamp. But their sounds are distinctive. The breeding call of the Indian nightjar resembles the sound of a stone skimming over the surface of a frozen pond; it can be heard for a considerable distance. Another species utters a loud grating call which, when close at hand, sounds exactly like a whiplash cutting the air. 'Horsfield's nightjar' (with which I am more familiar in Mussoorie) makes a noise similar to that made by striking a plank with a hammer.

I must not forget the owls, those most celebrated of night birds, much maligned by those who fear the night. Most owls have very pleasant calls. The little jungle owlet has a note which is both mellow and musical. One misguided writer has likened its call to a motorcycle starting up, but this is libel. If only motorcycles sounded like the jungle owl, the world would be a more peaceful place to live and sleep in.

Then there is the little scops owl, who speaks only in monosyllables, occasionally saying 'wow' softly but with great deliberation. He will continue to say 'wow' at intervals of about a minute, for several hours throughout the night.

Probably the most familiar of Indian owls is the spotted owlet, a noisy bird who pours forth a volley of chuckles and squeaks in the early evening and at intervals all night. Towards sunset, I watch the owlets emerge from their holes one after another. Before coming out, each puts out a queer little round head with staring eyes. After they have emerged, they usually sit very quietly for a time as though only half awake. Then, all of a sudden, they begin to chuckle, finally breaking out in a torrent of chattering. Having in this way 'psyched' into the right frame of mind, they spread their short, rounded wings and sail off for the night's hunting.

And I wend my way homewards. 'Night with her train of

stars' is always enticing. The poet Henley found her so. But he also wrote of 'her great gift of sleep', and it is this gift that I am now about to accept with gratitude and humility.

THE WALKERS' CLUB

Though their numbers have diminished over the years, there are still a few compulsive daily walkers around: the odd ones, the strange ones, who will walk all day, here, there and everywhere, not in order to get somewhere, but to escape from their homes, their lonely rooms, their mirrors, themselves...

Those of us who must work for a living and would love to be able to walk a little more don't often get the chance. There are offices to attend, deadlines to be met, trains or planes to be caught, deals to be struck, people to deal with. It's the rat race for most people, whether they like it or not. So who are these lucky ones, a small minority it has to be said, who find time to walk all over this hill station from morn to night?

Some are fitness freaks, I suppose; but several are just unhappy souls who find some release, some meaning, in covering miles and miles of highway without so much as a nod in the direction of others on the road. They are not looking at anything as they walk, not even at a violet in a mossy stone.

Here comes Miss Romola. She's been at it for years. A retired schoolmistress who never married. No friends. Lonely as hell. Not even a visit from a former pupil. She could not have been very popular.

She has money in the bank. She owns her own flat. But she doesn't spend much time in it. I see her from my window, tramping up the road to Lal Tibba. She strides around the mountain like the character in the old song 'She'll be coming round the mountain', only she doesn't wear pink pyjamas; she dresses in slacks and a shirt. She doesn't stop to talk to anyone. It's quick march to the top of the mountain, and then down again, home again, jiggety-jig. When she has to go down to Dehradun (too long a walk even for her), she stops a car and cadges a lift. No taxis for her; not even the bus.

Miss Romola's chief pleasure in life comes from conserving her money. There are people like that. They view the rest of the world with suspicion. An overture of friendship will be construed as taking an undue interest in her assets. We are all part of an international conspiracy to relieve her of her material possessions! She has no servants, no friends; even her relatives are kept at a safe distance.

A similar sort of character but even more eccentric is Mr Sen, who used to live in the US and walks from the Happy Valley to Landour (five miles) and back every day, in all seasons, year in and year out. Once or twice every week, he will stop at the Community Hospital to have his blood pressure checked or undergo a blood or urine test. With all that walking, he should have no health problems, but he is a hypochondriac and is convinced that he is dying of something or the other.

He came to see me once. Unlike Miss Romola, he seemed to want a friend, but his neurotic nature turned people away. He was convinced that he was surrounded by individual and collective hostility. People were always staring at him, he told me. I couldn't help wondering why because he looked fairly nondescript. He wore conventional western clothes, perfectly acceptable in urban India, and looked respectable enough except for a constant nervous turning of the head, looking to the left, right, or behind, as though to check on anyone who might be following him. He was convinced that he was being followed at all times.

'By whom?' I asked.

'Agents of the government,' he said.

'But why would they follow you?'

'I look different,' he said. 'They see me as an outsider. They think I work for the CIA.'

'And do you?'

'No, no!' He shied nervously away from me. 'Why did you say that?'

'Only because you brought the subject up. I haven't noticed anyone following you.'

'They're very clever about it. Perhaps you're following me too.'

'I'm afraid I can't walk as fast or as far as you,' I said with a laugh,' but he wasn't amused. He never smiled, never laughed. He did not feel safe in India, he confided. The saffron brigade was after him!

'But why?' I asked. 'They're not after me. And you're a Hindu with a Hindu name.'

'Ah yes, but I don't look like one!'

'Well, I don't look like a Taoist monk, but that's what I am,' I said, adding, in a more jocular manner: 'I know how to become invisible, and you wouldn't know I'm around. That's why no one follows me! I have this wonderful cloak, you see, and when I wear it, I become invisible!'

'Can you lend it to me?' he asked eagerly.

'I'd love to,' I said, 'but it's at the cleaners right now. Maybe next week.'

'Crazy,' he muttered. 'Quite mad.' And he hurried on.

A few weeks later, he returned to New York and safety. Then

I heard he'd been mugged in Central Park. He's recovering, but doesn't do much walking now.

Neurotics do not walk for pleasure, they walk out of compulsion. They are not looking at the trees or the flowers or the mountains; they are not looking at other people (except in apprehension); they are usually walking away from something—unhappiness or disarray in their lives. They tire themselves out, physically and mentally, and that brings them some relief.

Like the journalist who came to see me last year. He'd escaped from Delhi, he told me. He had taken a room in Landour Bazaar and was going to spend a year on his own, away from family, friends, colleagues, the entire rat race. He was full of noble resolutions. He was planning to write an epic poem or a great Indian novel or a philosophical treatise. Every fortnight I meet someone who is planning to write one or the other of these things, and I do not like to discourage them, just in case they turn violent!

In effect, he did nothing but walk up and down the mountain, growing shabbier by the day. Sometimes, he recognized me. At other times, there was a blank look on his face, as though he were on some drug, and he would walk past me without a sign of recognition. He discarded his slippers and began walking about barefoot, even on the stony paths. He did not change or wash his clothes. Then he disappeared; that is, I no longer saw him around.

I did not really notice his absence until I saw an ad in one of the national papers, asking for information about his whereabouts.

His family was anxious to locate him. The ad carried a picture of the gentleman, taken in happier, healthier times; but it was definitely my acquaintance of that summer.

I was sitting in the bank manager's office, up in the cantonment, when a woman came in, making inquiries about her husband. It was the missing journalist's wife. Yes, said Mr Ohri, the friendly bank manager, he'd opened an account with them; not a very large sum, but there were a few hundred rupees lying to his credit. And no, they hadn't seen him in the bank for at least three months

He couldn't be found. Several months passed, and it was presumed that he had moved on to some other town; or that he'd lost his mind or his memory. Then some milkmen from Kolti Gaon discovered bones and remnants of clothing at the bottom of a cliff.

In the pocket of the ragged shirt was the journalist's press card.

How he'd fallen to his death remains a mystery. It's easy to miss your footing and take a fatal plunge on the steep slopes of this range. He may have been high on something or he may simply have been trying out an unfamiliar path. Walking can be dangerous in the hills if you don't know the way or if you take one chance too many.

And here's a tale to illustrate that old chestnut that truth is often stranger than fiction.

Colonel Parshottam had just retired and was determined to pass the evening of his life doing the things he enjoyed most: taking early morning and late evening walks, afternoon siestas, a drop of whisky before dinner, and a good book on his bedside table.

A few streets away, on the fourth floor of a block of flats, lived Mrs L, a stout, neglected woman of forty, who'd had enough of life and was determined to do away with herself.

Along came the Colonel on the road below, a song on his lips, strolling along with a jaunty air; in love with life and wanting more of it.

Quite unaware of anyone else around, Mrs L chose that moment to throw herself out of her fourth-floor window. Seconds later she landed with a thud on the Colonel. If this was a Ruskin Bond story, it would have been love at first flight. But the grim reality was that he was crushed beneath her and did not recover from the impact. Mrs L, on the other hand, survived the fall and lived on into a miserable old age.

There is no moral to the story, any more than there is a moral to life. We cannot foresee when a bolt from the blue will put an end to the best-laid plans of mice and men.